NAOMI

OLIVE GURNEY

Beacon Hill Press of Kansas City
Kansas City, Missouri

Copyright 1992
by Beacon Hill Press of Kansas City

ISBN: 083-411-4399

Printed in the
United States of America

Cover Design: Crandall Vail
Cover Illustration: Keith Alexander

Unless otherwise indicated all Scripture quotations are from the *New American Standard Bible* (NASB), © The Lockman Foundation, 1960, 1962, 1963, 1968, 1971, 1972, 1973, 1975, 1977, and are used by permission.

10   9   8   7   6   5   4   3   2   1

Dedicated to my mother, Ernestine Hanna Lutes,
who directed me to the Savior
in my childhood and has been a continual
model of a woman committed to
knowing the Lord and His Word.

Preface

My attention was drawn to the woman Naomi through a class taught by my pastor's wife and my friend, Betty Jo Mathis. As we studied the Book of Ruth, I became increasingly interested in the person and life of Naomi, and thus the desire was born to share my thoughts with others in this book.

As I was writing the story of Naomi, I had several concerns. First, I wanted the book to be scripturally accurate, and I read and reread the Book of Ruth and related passages in the Bible in the endeavor to be true to the Word in every way possible.

Second, I have tried to make the story historically and culturally accurate. I have tried to show life as it really was in the period in which Naomi lived. Because the sources that I researched did not always agree, at times I had to choose between them.

But please understand that this is a novel, a work of fiction, based on a scriptural person. It is not intended as a Bible study book, and I have taken the liberty of giving the Bible characters personality traits and experiences that are not recorded in Scripture. For the factual account of Naomi's story, read the Book of Ruth in the Bible.

It is my prayer that this book will make Naomi a real person to you and that you will be blessed as you consider the Lord's dealings in her life.

1

*A*S SHE TRUDGED WEARILY along the road, Naomi's thoughts were far from the dusty journey that she was now making. She was thinking of another journey, made just 10 years ago—although it seemed in another lifetime.

I was so full of myself, she remembered. I was so sure that everything I wanted was waiting for me in Moab. I was a respected wife and mother, but still I was very young. Like a girl, I thought that those who had little deserved their plight because they did not try hard enough.

Naomi was abruptly brought back to the present as she stumbled on the path and Ruth's hand reached out to steady her. I am so tired and old! Her complaint was silent as she smiled her thanks to Ruth and continued in deep thought.

I never used to feel old, but defeat has such an aging effect. When I left Bethlehem with a noble husband and my two sons, I was full of energy. People marveled at the work I could do in a day, and I loved being busy. Cooking, sewing, managing the servants and Elimelech's house—every minute was full.

No one could say that Naomi's family was poorly fed or

clothed! she thought. Was this determination that people should think well of me where the problem began? Was I really proud and ambitious as old Cousin Leah accused me? Or was I just a diligent woman who was willing to work hard? I would prefer the second description, but I wonder if she was right. Whatever, it seemed to lead to my downfall.

I know that I was proud that Elimelech had chosen me to be his wife. He was so handsome and distinguished that I soon forgot my foolish daydreams of a young husband when he asked my father for my hand in marriage, Naomi remembered as her thoughts returned to the past.

How well I remember the evening when Father told me of his offer. It had been a hot summer day spent watching the sheep. Contentment filled my heart as I watched the animals through the long, drowsy afternoons. The sheep were content to graze quietly in the plentiful grass, and only occasionally did I need to retrieve a straying lamb. Twice I had to throw stones at hungry dogs who had threatened the flock. But few dangers existed in the gentle hills near Bethlehem where I kept the small portion of the flock for which I was responsible. The large flock was taken each summer to pasture much farther afield, and my father's hired shepherds had charge of them there.

And so I had time to dream—dreams of the house that would one day be mine, the husband who would find me the perfect homemaker, and the children that would come along to fill out the picture of bliss.

It was late afternoon that day when I brought in the sheep and our one milking goat. I sang and danced joyfully until I reached the outskirts of Bethlehem where I settled to the decorous walk of a young lady of virtue and maturity. But my heart was as light as the breeze that had begun to lift the oppressive heat of the day. Little did I know that my carefree life as a shepherdess had just come to an end.

Never since that day have I known that complete joy, Naomi reflected. For years I thought that particular quality of happiness existed only among the very young, but now I wonder. Is it possible that I could once more experience that pure happiness when I get back to the "place of blessing"? As I feel the gradual lifting of my burden, the memory of that marvelous happiness hums through my thoughts like a melody barely remembered. And again I feel the surge of hope. Perhaps it is never too late for joy—and perhaps I am foolishly hoping for the impossible.

That fateful evening Father did not look like a messenger of doom as he met me in the courtyard. His gentle face did have a curious stillness about it as he greeted me, "Peace be on you, Little One."

"And on you peace, my father," I replied automatically. "I have had such a good day, Father! You should have seen little Chelyah. She tried to stray away from the flock, and she looked so offended when I rescued her . . ." My voice trailed away. It was obvious that Father was paying me little heed. Indeed he only waited for my rush of words to cease before he spoke gravely.

"Naomi, I would speak with you. Let us go up to the roof where we may be alone."

Startled by his abrupt demeanor, I followed him up the narrow stairway to the roof. My heart thumped painfully in my breast as I waited for him to speak.

Because I was my father's youngest child and only daughter, our relationship was very different from that of other fathers and daughters. My father indulged me as much as possible, far more than was good for me according to Aunt Anna. He and I had spent much time together on our roof, but this was different, I could tell, and I watched him nervously.

Finally he cleared his throat and began to speak, "Naomi, my pleasant one, I have had an offer for you in marriage. And while to me you are still a little girl, your Aunt Anna has made me realize that it is time for you to be married . . ."

"Oh, Father, who has asked for me?" I interrupted. Even in the moments since he had begun to speak, I had envisioned several young men who might have sought my hand. Their glances in my direction had assured me of my beauty and desirability. Which one of them . . . ? Could it be Caleb? Oh, please let it be Caleb!

But Father was not to be hurried. "Now, Naomi, be quiet, Little One," but his voice was gentle. He looked at me measuringly, as if trying to assess just how grown up his little girl was.

"We are greatly honored, Naomi." He coughed, and I noticed again how uneasy he looked. Why, he is afraid to tell me! The thought flashed through my mind, and the knot within me grew tighter. But I remained silent as he groped for words to tell me my fate.

At last, evidently finding no way to soften the truth, he told me bluntly. "Elimelech came today and offered me a goodly sum as a bride-price for you. You must appear as lovely to him as you do to me, that he who is so honored among our people would desire you of all the maidens of Bethlehem."

I knew he was trying to encourage me, but the only response that could escape my stunned heart was an incredulous, "Elimelech?"

"Naomi," Father's voice was full of understanding. He hesitated a moment and then firmly began to extol the merits of the marriage. "Elimelech is a good man. He would never treat you cruelly. He is known throughout Bethlehem for his faith in the God of our fathers. He does not bow the knee to Baal or Ashteroth or any of the other foreign gods. And his faith has been tested and proven through the sorrow that he has borne.

"And besides that," my father continued doggedly, "Elimelech is wealthy. His flocks are large. He has a luxurious house and plenty of servants. You will have beautiful clothes and a position of honor as the wife of Elimelech."

My thoughts were a seething mass of rebellion as I listened. Well I knew that Elimelech was a good man, and wealthy too. He was even handsome. But none of that could compensate for his age. Why, he was surely nearing a score and ten.

"But, Father, he is old!"

My voice revealed my anguish although my eyes were dry. My tears seemed frozen in the icy lump within my breast.

Father enclosed me in a warm embrace. For a moment I felt his lips upon my forehead, and then he spoke close to my ear.

"My dear daughter, I realize that Elimelech seems old to you. But he is far from being an old man. Losing his wife and son in the Midianite raids added lines to his face and gray to his hair, but it also added compassion and gentleness to his heart.

"And also, Naomi," as he paused, he raised his hands to my shoulders and held me away from him, waiting until my eyes lifted to his own before continuing. "An older husband will be much better for you. You are strong-willed and spoiled, my Little One. You need a husband who will be firm with you, a man who will be your strong leader so that you will find happiness in your proper role as a submissive wife. You might find it all too easy to persuade a young man that your own way was best. But I am sure that Elimelech will not allow you to usurp his authority."

As he spoke, I realized that the decision had already been made. Of course, I thought bitterly, other fathers did not ask their daughters' opinions of a planned marriage, but I had assumed that I would be treated differently.

"As you will, my father," I responded stiffly.

Father's relief at my answer was apparent. He sounded more cheerful as he added, "Elimelech wants the betrothal ceremony to be right away; he suggested the 15th day of this month. That is only five days from now, but of course, we will have the year of your betrothal to prepare you for marriage and to assemble your dowry."

I nodded my head, thankful to have the date of my marriage far in the future. Perhaps my life could continue much as it had, and I could pretend that none of this was real.

But Father's next words ripped up that comforting thought. "No more will you be herding the sheep, Little One. Aunt Anna says it will take all of a year to teach you to be a proper housewife and mother in Israel. I am afraid that I have done wrong in letting you spend your days with the sheep instead of in the house helping with the women's work.

His last words were little more than a whisper, but I knew that my fate for the next year was sealed. No more would I roam the hills with the sheep or sit at my father's feet memorizing the Law. Aunt Anna had been aghast at those activities and repeatedly had told my father that I was receiving the attention normally given to a boy. But Father had resisted all her efforts to change our days' activities. He loved the Law and wanted to teach it, and I learned quickly and well. His eyes would shine with pride as I recited long portions of the Scriptures given to our fathers by Moses.

He had been thrilled when, as a little tot, I toddled after him when he went about his tasks with the sheep. Looking back, I realized that his loneliness for my mother had played a large part in my unusual upbringing. If she had lived, my childhood would have been very different. And I knew that if my brothers had been younger, nearer my own age, they would have filled his need for companionship. But they were grown men and busy tending their own flocks and herds, teaching their own children, while I was still very young. And so I had become my father's shadow and special pet.

But all that was finished. In the next year Aunt Anna would teach me what other girls had been learning all their lives. She would be a good teacher, no doubt. She ran the affairs of our household efficiently. And while she would be a stern taskmaster, she would not be unkind. But at the thought of days spent grinding barley and wheat, baking, spinning and weaving, the lump of ice in my breast threatened to burst into torrents of tears.

"Please may I now leave you, my father?" I gasped.

"Yes, Naomi, go in peace."

I fled down the stairs and out into the courtyard. In a dark corner, sheltered from sight by a tamarisk tree, I wept stormily for the loss of my dreams. When the tears were used up, I sat desolate, facing the bleakness of my future. I left my place of refuge only when called to join my family for the evening meal. And while I was thankful that the lamplight was pale and flickering so that my father could not really see my grief-ravaged face, I was able to speak with him in a normal enough fashion so that he expressed no concern.

I knew that Aunt Anna had discerned my distress, but she did not refer to it. She patted my shoulder kindly, however, as we rose from eating and directed, "I will see you in the courtyard at first light, Naomi. We will see what can be done about your training. Much will have to be done to prepare for your betrothal ceremony, so you can begin to learn the housewife's duties by helping with that."

"Yes, Aunt Anna," I replied quietly before slipping away to my pallet.

As I lay there that night, I tried to remember my mother. Although I had heard much about her—about her charm, her beauty, and her kindness, I had no real memories of her. She had died before I was weaned. But now, more than ever, I felt the need of a mother. Thinking of her, imagining her loving arms around me, brought me a measure of comfort, and I slept.

I awakened at first light to discover that the desolation

of the previous evening was gone. With renewed courage, I rose from my pallet to start my new life.

Those next few days gave me little time to regret the loss of my dreams, and I even began to feel a budding excitement as the preparations for the betrothal ceremony progressed. My best robe was carefully prepared; the veil, which would be lifted from my face and placed upon Elimelech's shoulder, must be absolutely immaculate. My long, dark hair and slender body were washed and scented until I did not even feel like the same girl who had sat on a hillside while the sheep nibbled grass nearby. I knew myself to be the center and object of all the hubbub, and that in itself was cheering.

* * *

The day of my betrothal arrived and was gone, and I wondered why there had been so much fuss for a ceremony that lasted only a few moments. That evening was unusually calm after the flurry of the last few days. I found myself unable to drift off into sleep. Although the betrothal ceremony had been very brief, I realized that now my life was changed irrevocably. I was committed to Elimelech for the rest of my life.

I was reminded afresh that from now on I must spin, weave, sew, grind, and cook like all the women I knew. And all for a man who had already had one wife, who would probably compare me unfavorably with her. How could I bear it? When I eventually slept, it was on a well-dampened pillow.

But the morning brought new courage, and I sought out Aunt Anna in the courtyard and urged her to teach me all that she knew. "I want to be the best housewife and mother in Israel," I told her, and she took me at my word.

The lessons continued throughout that trying year—trying for my aunt as well as for me. I was not always an apt pupil, but I was a very determined one, and as the months passed, I discovered that I did enjoy many of the duties of homemaking. Aunt Anna even praised my efforts and confided to my father that I was doing much better than she had expected.

Elimelech visited in our home nearly every week. At first I only watched and listened as he talked to my father. He seemed so solemn as they discussed the plight of our nation. Both men deplored the wickedness of the many people of Israel who worshiped the false gods of the Canaanites around us.

"You may be sure," my father declared, "that God will again send judgment. Right now our enemies are not attacking, and all seems to be going well, but God will not be mocked. We are in for serious trouble!"

"Yes, that is true," Elimelech agreed grimly. "And those who have remained true to Jehovah are bound to suffer with those who have not."

I did not like this talk of wickedness and suffering, so I shut out their words and turned to my own thoughts and dreams.

I was much more concerned with Elimelech's appearance than with his thoughts and conversation, Naomi remembered. As I assessed him, checking off good points and bad, I had to decide that his slow smile was the only aspect of his appearance that kept him from being ordinary. When he smiled, his whole face lightened and warmed.

I realized more and more that he was indeed a man to be admired, and I eagerly watched for the smiles he sent my direction.

At night upon my pallet I began to weave dreams of winning his admiration by proving myself the best housewife in Bethlehem. While I still mourned the death of my dreams, I began to anticipate the new life I would lead as his wife.

I had been at my housewife training only a few weeks when Aunt Anna began to send me to the well each morning for water. On my first trip to the well, the jar was heavy and awkward in my inexperienced hands. When I had finally gotten it onto my shoulder, I was exhausted and wondered how I would ever make the journey back to our house. Then I heard the words of old Elisheba, spoken more loudly than she realized because of her own deafness.

"Imagine a man of Elimelech's age and authority choosing a girl like that! She doesn't even know how to carry water! Can you imagine what her stew will taste like! Poor Anna has the impossible task of turning her into a proper housewife! I would not be surprised if even now Elimelech would realize his error and put her away!"

They are all laughing at me, I thought bitterly as I moved quickly out of earshot. "I'll show her—I'll show all of them!" I muttered.

The rest of the morning I ground the grain with such vigor that Aunt Anna laughingly protested, "Gently, Naomi. You will wear the stone down to nothing!"

Another distressing conversation occurred a few months later, Naomi remembered, and again it was at the well. Though the words were innocent and peaceful, they gave me even more hours of disquiet. By that time I was quite proficient at drawing and carrying water, and I had relaxed enough in my new duties to enjoy spending a little time chatting with the other girls of my own age who were also at the well to carry water to their houses.

That particular morning, I could tell that my friend Deborah was practically bursting with news as I watched her approach the well. Since we would both have to wait our turn at the well, I drew her away from the others.

"Come," I said, "you had better tell me quickly before you burst like an old wine skin that has been filled with new wine!"

She laughed joyously as she replied, "I, too, am to be betrothed, Naomi! Last night Caleb's father offered my father the bride-price. Our betrothal will take place next week.

Caleb has a nice flock now," she went on eagerly, "and he will build a little house for us. We will be poor, but I will be proud to help him become a rich and important man."

While I kept a smile on my face, my heart was sore. Caleb had always been my favorite of the young men of Bethlehem, and he had given me reason to think that he looked upon me with favor. When I had spent the hours in the hills dreaming of my future home, his was the face that had most often appeared in my dreams. Deborah's happy words drove the finality of my own betrothal home to me anew. When I was finally alone, my tears flowed freely.

But life went on, and the work continued. Aunt Anna was a thorough teacher and aimed to make me proficient in every area. One morning as I tried to spin an even thread, I protested to her, "Surely in the house of Elimelech I will have servants to do the difficult work. I could just let them do the spinning!"

But her answer was firm. "You must never expect your servants to do things better than you can do them yourself. And who knows—you may not always have servants to do your work."

I could see the sense of her first reason, but not the second. How thankful I am now that she taught me to do things for myself.

Only in the evenings, after all the tasks of the women were finished, did I have time to spend with Father. Together we would sit on the roof in warm weather, or close by the fire on chilly evenings, and Father would prepare me in his own way for marriage. One night he reminded me of the story of Sarah, the faithful, obedient wife of our father Abraham.

"Sarah is a good example for you to follow, my daughter. When Abraham went to Egypt, away from the land that God had given him, he directed Sarah to tell the Egyptians that she was his sister."

"But he was wrong to do that, wasn't he, Father?"

"Yes, Naomi, I believe that he was. But because Sarah obeyed her husband, God protected her. She did not understand, but she obeyed, and God always honors obedience, Little One. You must remember that."

Another evening he talked to me of Rebekah. "She started out so well. Like you, she had great courage, Naomi.

"Remember, my daughter, the Almighty God has said, 'Your husband ... shall rule over you.' You must submit to this rule, Naomi."

Father left the instructions regarding the marriage bed to Aunt Anna, who covered the subject as efficiently as she did everything else. No matter that she left no room for dreams of tenderness and romance. I had long ago given them up as connected with my own marriage.

Thus at the end of the year, prepared to the best of their combined abilities, I faced my marriage with some trepidation but also with a self-confidence that made me sure that whatever might happen, I would be able to cope.

* * *

As Naomi's mind hesitantly slipped back from the past to the present, she whispered, "I thank You, Lord God of Israel, that my father taught me the Scriptures while I was a child. For even though I did not allow them to shape my life then, when I finally realized that I could not cope with everything, I remembered that You could, and that You would help me."

2

▼▼▼▼▼

*T*HE DAY ON THE ROAD seemed very long. Naomi wondered if her strength would hold out until the journey's end at Bethlehem. Her daughter-in-law Orpah had tried to dissuade her from making the long trip, but Ruth had seemed to understand that she must go back to God's place of blessing.

"O my God," she breathed, "I have started this journey in obedience to You. I ask just as Jacob did so long ago that You 'will be with me and will keep me on this journey that I take.'"

Her step seemed lighter as she finished her prayer. She turned her eyes toward Ruth. The girl's eyes were shadowed with sadness, but her smile was warm and cheerful.

She had suffered so much as a bride, Naomi reflected. Even the first few months of her marriage were marred by the tension of living in the home of a foreigner. And there were only a few months of contentment before tragedy struck.

My own marriage was so different, Naomi remembered. Elimelech was such a kind, gentle husband. My happiness was of great importance to him. I am sure that his indulgent, peace-loving attitude contributed to our disastrous decision later on, and yet I know that most of the blame must rest squarely on my own shoulders.

It is still hard for me to understand why a man of his years yielded the reins of his life to a girl so inexperienced in life. I was only 14 when our marriage took place, but before the wedding feast was over, he had already deferred to my judgment.

It was the sixth day of the wedding feast that I first tasted the honeyed fruit of power. Those days of being the center of attention were the fulfillment of childish dreams. I could do no wrong. No one criticized my housekeeping skills—or anything else about me. As the bride of Elimelech, I enjoyed a new position of honor already.

And so as the end of the first seven days of feasting neared, I yearned to hold onto the pleasure of them longer. That evening as we sat together under the bridal canopy, I murmured, "Elimelech, my husband, must it all end after just one more day?"

He smiled, "It is the custom."

"But I remember Aunt Anna saying that when Jehoram was married, the feasting lasted for 14 days."

"Yes, that was quite a feast. We danced and sang as if sorrow could never touch our lives." For a moment his eyes were pensive, then he added, "But Jehoram was a very wealthy man."

A stab of jealousy pricked my heart. Elimelech would have been at Jehoram's wedding feast with his first wife, Helah.

But I quickly pushed those thoughts aside.

"You, my husband, are certainly not a poor man," I countered. But I smiled at him demurely as I spoke.

Sometime later, Elimelech asked, "Would you really want the feasting to go on for another week rather than settling down to our life together—just the two of us?"

"Oh, yes!" I exclaimed eagerly. "Why, we have years to

be settled down, but we can have only one wedding feast! Oh . . ." My voice trailed off miserably as I realized that this was Elimelech's second wedding feast.

But Elimelech acted as if he had heard nothing amiss. He patted my hand absently and then made his way to his cousin Reuben who served as governor of the feast. My surprise was as great as our guests' when Reuben signaled for silence.

"I have an announcement to make," his voice boomed out over the scattered chattering, "Elimelech has asked me to invite you to join with him in an additional seven days of feasting."

A shout of approbation rose from the crowd. The young people seemed overjoyed.

A few older people, however, raised their eyebrows. And I overheard someone say, "Not only will he empty his own coffers, but he will make us all poorer as well. I need my sons back in the hills watching the flocks."

How grumpy he is! I thought. I am glad my father does not begrudge his family a little fun!

But the following day when I expressed my outrage to my father, his face showed his concern.

"My dear daughter, you must understand that not everyone has enough servants to watch their sheep. Some have only their sons to help them, so they must do all the work themselves. You must be careful not to judge harshly when you do not know the facts, Little One."

Then he changed the subject and commented on the quality and quantity of the pomegranates that Elimelech had purchased from a passing caravan. But his words nibbled at my happiness throughout the remaining seven days of feasting.

As I observed our guests, it seemed that their gaiety was forced. And my own pleasure was dimmed. As Aunt Anna had occasionally commented, "Even the tastiest of fruits begins to pall when one has eaten to the full!"

And so I am sure that it was a relief to all concerned when the wedding feast was finally over, and we settled down to normal living.

But the pattern of that one area of our lives had begun to form. Elimelech seldom denied me my desires. I must say that my wishes were generally meant to be helpful, and I thought that my way was better for everyone.

I was happy that first year of our marriage. I adapted easily to managing a house on my own. Our house was one of the finest in Bethlehem. My father's house was made up of two rooms with the courtyard between and so was considered more than adequate. But Elimelech's house consisted of three rooms—one on each side of the courtyard. Atop the center room, the roof was enclosed to give privacy to our summer sleeping quarters. The house was the most visible sign of Elimelech's wealth.

I found pleasure in keeping our household running smoothly. I kept the servants busy from morning till night so that Elimelech would be pleased.

Elimelech left the house early each day to oversee the work with the sheep. He spent considerable time at the city gates, hearing problems and legal matters brought to the respected men who sat there. It would often be dusk when he returned home. The hours seemed long with him gone, but being busy helped speed the days.

Another reason for my industry was less praiseworthy. Elimelech's cousin Leah had angered me in the early days of our marriage by commenting on my carefree childhood and by advising me, "I do hope you will try not to be an embarrassment to Elimelech. He has an important position in Bethlehem, and it is a pity that he did not choose his second wife more wisely. Perhaps if you will let me teach you, I can help you to become an adequate housewife."

Icily I had rejected her help, saying, "My Aunt Anna has taught me well, and I am sure that I shall manage."

As soon as the words were out of my mouth, I knew

that I had offended her, but pride kept me from apologizing. I did, however, wonder if she really had meant to be kind with her poorly worded offer.

So to prove my point I felt that I had to keep a perfect house. Her visits were times of great tension since I was sure she was always looking for something to criticize.

A few months after our marriage I conceived. I had no idea of my capacity for motherhood. But as soon as I suspected that I was with child, I felt great anticipation.

And Elimelech's pride in the coming event was a delight to me. I had no bouts of vomiting as so many women did, and that added to my self-satisfaction. I was eager for the opportunity to tell Cousin Leah. At least now, I thought triumphantly, she cannot criticize the speed with which I became with child!

The months sped by in spite of my eagerness. When the first pain hit, I rejoiced and waited eagerly for more before sending servants to notify Elimelech and to fetch Aunt Anna. Elimelech arrived first, and his nervousness and joy mixed would have been amusing had I been in less pain.

"My dear, what can I do for you? Has your Aunt Anna been summoned? Are you sure I should not call another midwife to help her? Oh, when will she come? Perhaps I should go fetch her myself!"

Again and again, closer and closer the pain surged through my body. Suddenly I was frightened. I, who had never feared childbirth, felt myself falling to the level of those women who screamed in terror at the onset of travail.

I nearly wept with relief when Aunt Anna bustled in and sent Elimelech from the room. Her sensible words helped me keep my perspective as she made all the preparations.

"So this is the day that you become a mother, Naomi!" she congratulated. "And like everything else you do, you travail with all your might! At this rate it will be no time at all until the child is born."

And after a time my son was born. Oh, Mahlon, my firstborn, how beautiful you were to your mother! Naomi thought as the bittersweet memories of her first son's birth flowed over her.

I was wrapped up in the joy of holding my own child when I heard Aunt Anna's voice speaking to someone in the doorway. "It is a man child, and she has had a very easy birthing."

"God be praised!" I heard Elimelech's fervent exclamation. I smiled at Elimelech as he came hesitantly into the room, closely followed by Cousin Leah.

Elimelech tiptoed to my pallet and knelt down to look at his son. Then he bent and kissed my forehead gently. "Thank you, my wife," he whispered. "God has blessed our union and given me an heir." With one large finger, he carefully touched his son's little hand.

It was then that Cousin Leah came up close and uttered the words that filled me with fury and fear. "He looks puny! And notice how blue he is. I hope that he will live, Elimelech."

Perhaps she was only trying to warn us of the possibility of a sickly baby's early death, but to me her words were as cruel as a whip upon my tender heart.

"Do you really think he is not well?" Elimelech asked her fearfully, and at her grim nod, he turned to Aunt Anna.

But she, too, bowed her head in sorrowful confirmation of Cousin Leah's assessment.

"He is small, and his color is bad, but babies can outgrow those conditions with good care. And I am sure that Naomi will give him excellent care." Aunt Anna lifted her face to give me an encouraging smile.

"We will call him Mahlon," my husband said tersely, "and hope that we can change his name as he grows older."

At his words my heart grew chill. Elimelech, too, believed that our baby was not healthy and so had given him the name Mahlon, meaning "sick." I closed my eyes to hide my pain from all of them and clutched my baby more tightly. To my relief they left the room quietly, and I again opened my eyes to look at my sleeping son.

"Your name is Mahlon for now, my child, but it will change; it must! You are my beloved son, and with my good care you will soon be strong and well. We will change your name to Azaz when you are strong and healthy." And cheered by my own determined words, I drifted off to sleep.

I quickly regained my strength and anxiously watched over my baby, willing him to be healthy and strong. I tried to convince myself that the two older women's warnings were just pessimism. But I kept my thoughts to myself, fearful that they might not see as much improvement as I did.

I was able to keep up my pretense for several months, but then my little Mahlon became really sick. His body was hot as I held him in my arms; his breathing was quick and shallow, and he coughed and gasped for breath. Aunt Anna came and together we fought for my son's life.

Elimelech tried to comfort and encourage me, but I had no time to listen to his comforting words. My thoughts were only for my son.

Miraculously, the baby pulled through, but that was only the first of many battles for his life.

Although I never gave up on Mahlon's becoming healthy, I did look forward eagerly to having other babies. So when I discovered that I was again with child, my heart rejoiced. Again my time of waiting passed uneventfully while I enjoyed good health.

The only untoward events that marred those months of waiting were the bouts of fever that attacked little Mahlon. But these attacks were seldom as bad as the first one, and I had learned to give him the best care.

Although Mahlon was smaller than other children his age, he did talk young, so we knew that the fevers had not affected his mind. He was a bright child, and I determined that someday we would see him strong.

Then the travail came announcing the day of my second child's birth—or so I supposed until the day passed, leaving me still in the midst of my pain. I could tell that Aunt Anna was concerned although she gave me only encouraging words. "Some babies are not eager to come into this world. But he will come. He will find out soon that his mother will not be denied!"

But the long stretches of the night passed, and my strength was waning badly. I began to drift into unconsciousness when a pain eased, only to be brought instantly alert when another tore through my body.

The second day Aunt Anna called in another midwife, and eventually, after both of them had worked over me throughout the afternoon, my second son was born.

During those long, difficult hours, Aunt Anna had repeated several times, "Surely he must be a big healthy boy!"

But he was not. According to the second midwife, the trouble had been caused by his position rather than his size. Again I had given birth to a small, sickly son. And although I did not know it yet, I would never again bear a child. I am glad that I did not know, Naomi reflected.

I felt that I had more than I could bear as first Aunt Anna and then Cousin Leah looked at my baby and shook their heads sadly.

"But surely he is all right?" I whispered. But as Aunt Anna's eyes filled with tears, I knew that I had her answer.

This time my recovery was slow, and those who cared for me feared for my life as I battled fever and weakness. But in time I recovered enough to again take over the care of my two little sons. Our new baby was named Chilion, meaning "pining."

And the next time Mahlon became ill, only a few days passed before tiny Chilion developed the same symptoms. And while caring for one sick little boy had filled all my hours and taxed my strength, now I must care for two.

To make matters worse, my father became ill, and Aunt

Anna was needed to care for him. I did not know how I could go on.

Poor Elimelech! During those days, I ignored him and concentrated completely on my sons, Naomi remembered sadly. A less patient man would not have put up with my snapping responses, but he did his best to help me and tried to get me to rest, leaving the servants to cope for a few hours.

One day when I had reached the end of myself, he insisted that I lie down. "The servants will care for our sons. You must rest or you will be sick, too, my beloved."

Even in my distress, his endearment warmed my heart, but with tears pouring down my cheeks, I sobbed, "But they are my sons. I think sometimes that only my love pulls them through."

"Then I will watch over them myself," he answered as he led me to my pallet in a quiet part of the house.

When I awoke a few hours later, it was to find Elimelech holding the sleeping Mahlon in his arms while Cousin Leah walked the floor with fretful little Chilion. Cousin Leah smiled at me uncertainly, and I knew that she was unsure of her welcome, but her presence was reassuring, and I felt my burden lift a bit.

That first time that Cousin Leah helped us out she made sure that I understood that she was only staying until the babies were well again. However, as one sickness followed another, Cousin Leah spent more time with us than in her own house. Within a few months our home became hers, and she spoke no more of returning to her house.

Life was difficult with Cousin Leah in the house. I knew that she thought it was my fault that the babies were not strong.

"Elimelech's first son," she informed me, "was a strong, sturdy child."

But at least, I thought rebelliously, my sons are alive. Elimelech's son and his mother had been killed in a Midianite raid when the boy was 12 years old. Elimelech had waited over 4 years before asking my father for me as his second wife.

Even with Cousin Leah there to help carry the load, I was always tired, always tense. When the babies were sick, my energy came from my fear for them. And when they were well, I lived in dread of the next illness. One night I wept in Elimelech's arms, "How long? How long can this go on? I cannot take any more!" And his tears flowed with mine as he held and comforted me.

* * *

Now Naomi found her eyes full of tears as she thought of Elimelech. Surreptitiously she wiped her eyes with the sleeve of her robe, but Ruth had seen the tears, and her warm clasp of Naomi's hand showed her own love and understanding.

"Thank You, Lord, that You have shown me Your love through both of these dear people—first through Elimelech, and now through my Moabite daughter-in-law. And, Lord God, may she also feel Your love through me." Not even her lips moved as Naomi offered her thanks to God.

3

▼▼▼▼▼

AHLON WAS IN HIS FIFTH YEAR and Chilion his third when it happened. Elimelech
had suggested that I go to Shiloh with him to
celebrate the Feast of Tabernacles. My first and very definite
response was, "No. How can you even think that I would
leave our sons!"

His quiet reply had horrified me even further. "We will
take them with us. Not," he added quickly as he saw the
look in my eye, "if they are sick at the time. But if they are
not, it would do them good to be out and see a bit of our
world." Then without giving me a chance to argue further,
Elimelech had changed the subject, and he did not mention
the idea again for several days.

But it was never far from my mind. "How I would love
to go to Shiloh! But if the boys were not sick when we left,
they surely would be before we got back. Yet, they have had
periods longer than the days needed for the trip without
sickness. My thoughts ran in circles, giving me no peace, so
finally when Elimelech brought up the subject again, I did
not need much persuading.

He said firmly to me, "Naomi, I think that we should go to Shiloh as a family."

It was a relief to me to settle the question, and I replied, "Yes, if the boys are well when the day comes, I will go."

Oh, the hubbub as we prepared for the trip! Mahlon and Chilion responded to the bustle with mounting excitement. All of the excitement brought the inevitable result, and the day before we were to leave, both were fretful and cranky.

Well, that's it, I thought gloomily, we will have to stay home. Tears of self-pity and frustration soaked my pillow that night.

But by morning there was no sign of the dreaded fever, and we set off to join the crowd of travelers from our area of Judah, all headed for Shiloh and the feast.

Elimelech had fixed special baskets on our donkey, and when the boys tired, they rode contentedly in their baskets. They were often lulled to sleep by the gentle rocking of their baskets.

In their baskets the boys stood the trip well, and I began to enjoy chatting with the other young mothers. I began to realize how badly I had needed this break from my worries.

On the fourth day of our traveling we arrived at Shiloh. There we found many others from all the 12 tribes of Israel also gathering. The air was full of shouts of greeting and joyous laughter as pilgrims met and greeted others they had not seen for at least a year.

That first evening was devoted to preparing our booths for this Feast of Tabernacles. The purpose of the feast was originally to remind us of God's delivering us from bondage and His provision for our people while they lived over 40 years out in the wilderness. Later on the custom had been added of celebrating the bountiful harvest in the land to which God had brought us—the land promised to our father Abraham.

On the next day, the first day of the feast, we all stood for many hours listening as a priest read the Law. I was amazed at how well-behaved the children were while we heard the Torah read.

The rest of the days of the feast would be spent in celebration. Each morning, however, sacrifices were offered.

On the fourth day, my carefree, joyous fling was ruined. While Chilion normally stayed quite close to me rather than join his brother and the other little boys who played farther afield, his eyes had until that time been bright with interest, observing all the new and strange happenings. But as the heat of the day passed, I noticed that his cheeks were unnaturally flushed and that his eyes had the glazed look of fever. When I laid my hand on his forehead, my foreboding was justified. My joy was gone as though it had never been. Now we would fight a bout with the fever while living in a booth four days' journey from home. Perhaps Elimelech could find someone in Shiloh who would allow us to stay in their house. It was not commanded that women and small children live in booths during the feast, but we had wanted to be with Elimelech and enjoy the novelty of sleeping under the stars.

I quickly carried Chilion into the little booth and laid him on his mat. First I needed cold water—not the lukewarm water that I had on hand. Stepping to the open side of the booth, I spotted Mahlon, now resting on the grass after his play. He came at my call and started off, listlessly following my instructions that he find Cousin Leah and bring her quickly.

When he returned to the booth with her, I left her to watch both boys and hurried off to the well. I was the only one drawing water at this time of day, so there was no waiting, and I was soon on my way back.

Upon reentering the booth, I found Cousin Leah gently rocking Chilion. "Thank you, Cousin Leah, I will look after him now. I want to bathe him with cool water," and I took him from her arms.

How it hurt me when Chilion resisted me, whimpering, "No! Want Cousin Eah!" And while I held him, he began to cry in earnest.

Yielding, I put him back into her arms and turned away, my own eyes filled with tears. My own son preferred another to me. Surely she must have been trying to win my sons away from me. The hurt quickly began to sour into bitterness. "Since I am not needed here," I steadied my voice to say, "I will go to the Tabernacle to pray for my son."

I do not remember meeting anyone on the way to the Tabernacle, although the whole town was thronged with people. But my eyes were dim with tears, and my thoughts were in turmoil as I hurried along.

When I reached the Tabernacle, I slipped in quietly and found a spot where I could be alone. There I poured out my heart to the Lord. "O God," I cried, "my sons! I have done all that I know to do, and they are still sickly. And now they are turning away from me! (I realize now that this was not really true, but in my anguish, it seemed so then.) O Lord God, I know that You are all-powerful. Since You brought our whole nation through the Red Sea with dry feet, I know You could give my sons good health. And what could be too hard for a God who made the sun stand still?"

I continued on for some time, pleading with the Lord for health for my sons until eventually I realized that evening was drawing near. Then I slipped away with a lighter heart and retraced my way to our temporary shelter.

I found the family gathered there, and I was amazed to sense a spirit of rejoicing.

"How is Chilion?"

The words had barely passed my lips before they were telling me that Chilion's fever was gone. "He is well, Mother," shouted Mahlon, "and he is hungry! And so am I," he added, making sure that I got the message.

Indeed I could see a remarkable change in Chilion's appearance. He certainly did appear to be well. He was bouncing on his father's lap, laughing boisterously at the game that they had been playing.

Suddenly my joy was back. God was good, and life was sweet. Then I realized that Mahlon was sitting on Cousin Leah's lap. He seemed completely at home there, and again I felt my heart wrench with jealousy.

Later that night as Elimelech and I lay close together on our pallets, I looked up at the stars through the gaps in the branches over our heads. My heart was full of the experiences of the day, things that I must share with my husband.

"You know, I went to the Tabernacle to pray for our sons today," I whispered. "I asked Jehovah to heal them. Do you think that He has answered my prayer?" Without waiting for his answer, I rushed on. "Never before has either of our sons recovered so quickly from a fever—and Chilion really did have a fever! He was just burning up!" My words ran together in my need to convince both Elimelech and myself.

"I do not know," was Elimelech's cautious answer. "We will just have to wait and see. At any rate, he certainly does seem to be well now."

I was not satisfied with his reply although it was obviously the truth. Patience and waiting never came easily for me.

The second subject that I wished to discuss was more difficult to broach, and it was some time before I asked, "Have you noticed that Cousin Leah is turning our sons against me?"

"What?" he murmured sleepily.

I repeated my question, and he hesitated so long before answering that I was sure he had drifted off to sleep.

"No, I have not noticed anything of the kind," he finally replied. "What makes you think such a thing?"

"Just things I have noticed." I evaded, warned by the tone of his voice. And I dropped the subject for the moment.

Chilion was not ill in the morning. Indeed his strength seemed increased for the remainder of our days at Shiloh. He even began to run and play with other boys his size. I am sure no mother ever watched her children more hopefully, looking for any sign that could be construed to show good health.

And both of my sons did improve! The cycle of those debilitating fevers was broken. But whatever it was that caused them to become so easily tired, that kept them pale and breathless—that never completely went away. So although my life was much easier and more peaceful, I did not feel satisfied that God had completely answered my prayer.

During the remainder of our days at Shiloh, I still was jealous of Cousin Leah's place in their affections.

Then an overheard conversation settled my resolve to see Elimelech's cousin out of our home.

I had no intention of eavesdropping when I heard those words that angered me so deeply. I had left our booth, telling Cousin Leah that I would be visiting in the booth of my friend Deborah while she and the boys rested. As I left our shelter, I met an old friend of Cousin Leah's going to chat with her. We exchanged greetings, and both hurried on our way.

But as I approached Deborah's booth, I realized that I had left my embroidery behind, so impatiently I retraced my steps. Nearing our booth, I heard Cousin Leah's friend ask, "Don't you miss living in your own house? You are little more than a servant in the house of Elimelech!"

I paused, taken aback that others should think that we treated Cousin Leah like a servant.

Then Cousin Leah began to speak, and I stood rooted for some moments. "Yes, I miss my own house, but Naomi just could not care for her family without me. You know she had no proper upbringing, and things were getting beyond her. Once she scorned my offer of help, but when Elimelech came begging me to help them out, I did not stand on my pride. I went to them immediately. And now it is as though these little ones were my own sons."

"No," I gasped, and suddenly I could bear to hear no more. As I turned away, my thoughts were in a whirl of self-justification. The only reason that I could not handle my family was that I had two desperately sick sons, I fumed inwardly. No one could be expected to handle that alone. And I certainly will handle them alone from now on! Her sons indeed!

A second time I was stumbling through Shiloh without seeing anything or anyone. Suddenly a firm hand grasped my arm, and a familiar voice laughingly asked, "Where are you going in such a rush?"

"Oh, Elimelech, I have to talk to you!" And to my shame, my lips began to quiver, and tears spilled down my cheeks.

The laughter was gone from his voice as he gently led me away. "Come with me, my love. We will find a place that is a bit less public."

Desperately I fought for control, not wishing to be a public spectacle, until we reached a quiet spot, sheltered by terebinth trees. There my frustrations and hurt poured forth, and I told him my story, quite incoherently, I fear. But Elimelech's gentle questions eventually drew out the conversation that I had heard.

"But, of course, Leah loves our sons. She has never had children, and she is overjoyed to have a share in ours. But she could never steal your place even if she wanted to, and I am sure that she does not."

"She must go back to her own home," I insisted stubbornly. "She said that she missed her own house. And if the boys are really healed, then I will not need her help!"

Elimelech looked at me with gentle reproach, but said only, "We will have to wait and see."

"But not too long!" I added, determined that I would have my way in this.

And in less than a month's time after our return to Bethlehem, Cousin Leah was in her own little house. I had been very polite and pleasant but also very determined.

"Now that my sons are in better health," I had suggested, "I am sure that you would like to return to your own house. When Elimelech asked you to help, he did not realize that their sickness would drag on so long. But now I can manage and you should be able to live more quietly. The boys are getting so noisy now that they are more healthy!" I ignored the stunned expression in Cousin Leah's eyes.

"But my house," she demurred at last, "I am sure that it is in disrepair after all this time."

"Yes, but I will see to it that everything is made ready for you. It will sparkle when I am finished! And after you have moved home, I will send Mahlon and Chilion over to visit often and to bring you good things from our table." How gracious I could be if I could just have my own way!

Immediately I set to work getting her house restored, personally overseeing the work and making sure that it did indeed sparkle. Somehow Elimelech heard nothing of the plan until the night before his cousin was to return to her home. I had never had the courage to tell him what I had done and did not really want him to know until things had passed the point of no return. But someone mentioned to him the flurry of work being done on Cousin Leah's house, and the damage was done.

Elimelech's face was grave as he entered our house and called me aside. "What is this I hear of Cousin Leah's house being prepared for occupancy? What have you done?"

I found it very difficult to meet his eyes, but I answered boldly, "She missed being in her own home, but she was worried that it was in too bad of shape to be livable. So I have sent servants to do repair and make it clean and comfortable for her."

"Does she really want to go?" His voice was so stern that my heart quaked.

"You can ask her for yourself," I replied in a hurt voice.

"I will," he said curtly and left to find his cousin.

I could not help it; I had to follow. But Cousin Leah's answer to his question relieved my fear and, also, made me feel ashamed. "Yes, I go to my own house willingly. Naomi has been very kind in preparing it for me." She looked up and caught my eye as I stood partly hidden behind the door post, and I knew that I had not deceived her as to my purpose.

And on the next day she moved. I had refused to recognize the loneliness that I saw in her eyes. Instead I busied myself with good deeds toward her although I rarely visited her myself. I sent Mahlon or Chilion to carry the gifts of my bounty. Gradually my conscience pained me less. I had almost convinced myself that I had really done Cousin Leah a favor, forgetting that my motive had been to see her out of my house.

*   *   *

Naomi's thoughts were abruptly brought back to the present when the shout passed down the straggly line of travelers that the caravan had reached the spot chosen for that night's camp.

Later, as she helped get ready for the night, searching for bits of wood or dried sheep dung for their fire, she whispered, "O Lord God, the Almighty One, I would that Cousin Leah may still be alive when I return to Bethlehem. I must admit my fault to her. O Lord, would You lengthen her days so that I might speak to her? And I thank You, Lord, that my daughters-in-law have treated me with kindness rather than after the fashion of my own unkindness to Elimelech's cousin."

4

NAOMI AND RUTH were now three days' journey
from Kir-haraseth where they had joined the
caravan. The journey was not one for the faint-
hearted even though they walked the King's Highway, a
well-traveled trade route. Yesterday they had forded the Ar-
non River. Later they would ford the much larger Jordan.
Naomi would certainly be ready to sleep when she could finally stretch out upon her mat in the little tent that she
shared with Ruth.

But tired as she was, Naomi knew that she would
awaken sometime during the night and lie awake for a long
time with past and future events crowding her mind. Long
ago she had reconciled herself to these long night watches,
and now she almost welcomed the quiet time alone to reflect and pray.

The evening's work was eventually finished, and the
camp became quiet. Naomi and Ruth were both soon asleep.

As she had expected, Naomi awoke while the moon
was still high in the sky. She lay quietly, listening to Ruth's
even breathing. She is so young, Naomi thought, so young to
face a new country and a new people—even younger than I

was when we made the trip to Moab. But she is full of courage in facing the difficulties of a new life.

I did not possess her wisdom. To me the move was a grand adventure, and I was sure that it would be the answer to all our troubles.

Of course, I had never dreamed of leaving Bethlehem before the famine struck. But the winter rains stopped coming. The grass dried up, so Elimelech's shepherds had to take the sheep farther and farther away from home. The wheat and barley shriveled and died.

How the east wind blew that first year of the drought! Instead of lasting only a day or two as it did normally, it continued over a week. Day after day the sky was leaden. People and animals coughed and choked from the dust in the air. I watched my sons in anxiety, but they withstood the terrible conditions better than I had feared.

But it was not during that summer that I began to desire to move away. I was sure the next year would be better —the rains would come again, and the barley and wheat would again produce a bountiful crop.

But the rains did not come. The months of winter passed with relief from the heat but no refreshing rains. Even at the end of winter, when the latter rains were expected, there was nothing.

It was then, facing a second long, hot summer that I began to be discouraged. It was not that we were starving. We had sheep to eat, and by selling a few of them, we could buy grain from the merchant caravans. But the grain brought in this way was very expensive. And there were no fresh vegetables or fruit available, and I worried lest our sons should sicken on this poorer diet. Also I knew that our flock would dwindle as we had to sell more and more sheep to buy our supplies.

Then one day while I was buying grain from the caravan, I overheard a traveler say, "What a difference between the east side of the Jordan and the west! In Moab all is green and lush, but here everything is dry and brown."

Moab—the land was not far away, but a trip there would take time. The people of Moab were our enemies and were despised by all good Israelites. But they were peaceful. Surely they would not harm a family come to stay awhile.

That evening I mentioned to Elimelech, "Today I heard a trader say that the drought has not touched Moab. Only a few miles east of us the country is green and beautiful!"

Elimelech looked older than his years, and his voice held weariness as he replied, "Yes, I have heard the reports. But God is not judging Moab. It is Israel He will judge. He warned our forefathers that it would be so if we did not obey Him.

"But our people will not listen. They will worship the gods of the Canaanites or the Amorites or whatever god promises the most." His voice was bitter, and I knew that I was not the first one to hear him speak these words. My father had told me that Elimelech had angered many by his charges of their own responsibility for this famine.

"Naomi," he had said, "you have a husband to be proud of. I know it is not easy for Elimelech to speak out, but he has taken a stand for the God of our fathers. If only our people would listen."

"But, Father," I responded, "not all of us worship idols. Why should we suffer with the rest!"

"Speak not, my daughter, of fair or unfair. Instead pray for our land, and search your own heart. Remember, Moses gave us the remedy for times like these. 'Then the Lord your God will prosper you abundantly in all the work of your hand, in the offspring of your body and in the offspring of your cattle and in the produce of your ground, for the Lord will again rejoice over you for good, just as He rejoiced over your fathers; if you obey the Lord your God to keep His commandments and His statutes which are written in this book of the law, if you turn to the Lord your God with all your heart and soul.'

"Remember, Naomi, not all other gods are made of wood and stone. Some may be made of flesh. Oh, yes, we deserve the famine. The Lord has warned us," he again began to quote from the Law, "'Now it shall be, if you will diligently obey the Lord your God, being careful to do all His commandments which I command you today, the Lord your God will set you high above all the nations of the earth. And all these blessings shall come upon you and overtake you, if you will obey the Lord your God. Blessed shall you be in the city, and blessed shall you be in the country. Blessed shall be the offspring of your body and the produce of your ground and the offspring of your beasts, the increase of your herd and the young of your flock.'"

As I listened to his voice rolling out the words of blessing, my mind drifted back to the days when I had sat at his knee and memorized these promises. But then Father finished reciting the blessings and continued on into the curses. As he reached the ones that particularly pertained to our situation, my attention was caught. "And the heaven which is over your head shall be bronze, and the earth which is under you, iron. The Lord will make the rain of your land powder and dust; from heaven it shall come down on you until you are destroyed."

I waited until my father finished his quotation and then rose to take my leave. I bent to kiss him and say farewell, but his mind was far from me, and he did not notice my departure.

Now as Elimelech spoke, I remembered my father's words. "But I worship no foreign gods, and I see no reason why my family should suffer with those who do!" I kept these thoughts to myself.

In the days that followed, I spent many hours pondering the words of the Law. Another portion of that passage that Father had quoted had not struck me that day at his house, but now it echoed in my mind. "The Lord will smite you with consumption and with fever and with inflammation and with fiery heat and with the sword and with blight and with mildew, and they shall pursue you until you perish."

Could this also apply? Were my sons' illnesses a curse from the Almighty because of disobedience? But I do not worship Baal or any of the other heathen idols.

Father's words slipped into my thoughts, "Remember, Naomi, not all other gods are made of wood and stone. Some may even be made of flesh."

Did he think I worshiped my sons? Ridiculous! I only loved my sons as a mother should! But the words haunted me, and I vowed to discuss it with him on my next visit.

But that visit never took place. Father died in his sleep the night before I was to make my weekly trip to his home.

My first reaction to his death was of shock and, amazingly, anger. I needed him! How could he be dead? It was not until after the wailing procession to the tomb that true grief filled my heart. Before that my wails had been no more genuine than those of the hired mourners.

But, when I slipped away from the house to the privacy of the hills outside Bethlehem, I found myself engulfed in the anguish of his loss. Then I wept.

When I returned home, I could once more face the relatives and friends who had come to mourn with us.

Father's death left a large gap in my life. No longer did his counsel temper my thoughts and actions. I know now that I should have looked to Elimelech as my guide, but somehow, I never saw him as the wise leader that he was.

Thoughts of the benefits of a trip to Moab were now my daily company. "In Moab we would not be choking on dust." Or, "In Moab we would have fresh fruit." The list grew and slipped out bit by bit in my conversation.

One hot, trying day I stormed in Mahlon's hearing, "The east wind is not blowing like this in Moab."

He looked at me in surprise and then asked, "Is Moab a better land than this, Mother?"

"At the moment," I returned shortly.

"Tell me about Moab."

His dark eyes, normally twinkling, were now serious and determined. "Tell me," he repeated imperiously.

"Moab is the land east of the Jordan River," I began. "It is well protected from enemies by surrounding hills and the cliffs along the river and by the Salt Sea. The land is fertile, and the rains come. The barley and wheat produce good harvests, and the sheep are fat."

"But what of the people?" he interrupted. "Are they our friends or our enemies?"

I hesitated and then answered carefully. "They are our distant relatives. You remember that your father has told you of Abraham and his nephew Lot. We, of course, are the descendants of Abraham, and they are from the family of Lot."

"But are they our friends?" he persisted.

"Not exactly. They have never fought against our people, but they refused to allow our nation to travel through their land as we came out of Egypt. And they tricked and defiled our people. But they are peaceful, and they do not attack and raid as many of our neighbors do."

"Hmmm," he paused, then added seriously, "but all is green there—and cool?"

At my nod he turned away, and I smiled to see him so seriously considering the problem.

However, I did not smile when he asked Elimelech, "Father, would we be wise to go to Moab until the famine has passed?"

Elimelech's eyes met mine, and I knew that he understood where Mahlon had come up with the idea. "No, Son, I do not think that would be wise. *This* is the land that God gave us, and *this* is where we belong whether in plenty or in famine." Again he looked at me steadily until my own eyes wavered and fell.

But later I defended myself against his unspoken accusations. "Mahlon asked me to tell him about Moab, and I did. I did not tell him that I thought we should go there."

"But you do think so, do you not?"

I hesitated only a moment before answering. "Would it be so terrible to live there just until this famine passes? Our father Abraham went to Egypt twice in like circumstances."

"Yes," he retorted, "and he got into trouble both times!"

"But our sheep are going to starve if this continues. We shall be penniless."

Elimelech just sighed and turned over on his pallet.

As the drought continued, I began to mention Moab longingly in Elimelech's presence. The first few times that I did so, I watched him closely for signs of anger. But he only looked thoughtful, so I grew bolder.

One morning when Elimelech had started to leave the house, I walked outside with him. Together we stood looking at the brazen sky. "Oh, will it never rain?" he groaned.

"Elimelech," I sympathized, "I hate to see all your work done for naught and your flocks dwindle to nothing. Could you not make inquiries about conditions in Moab and the possibility of moving there until the Lord again sends rain on our homeland?"

He patted my hand as he answered, "I have instructed Abel who travels with a caravan to check out the possibilities in Moab as they travel through. He is to bring me word within the month. But that does not mean," he added, "that I am convinced that we should leave our land. I just thought it would be as well to learn about the situation there."

"Oh, Elimelech, you are so wise and patient! I am sure you will make the right decision!"

Secretly I began to plan for the move. As I cooked, I

decided which pots and utensils must go with us and which should be left to be replaced in Moab.

And always I listened for news of Moab. I even found myself wanting to defend Moab's people when my Israelite neighbors expressed anger or scorn.

Eagerly I awaited the return of the caravan. News traveled fast in our small town, and the arrival of the merchants with their goods from far away was news indeed.

Then one evening word was passed that a caravan was approaching. They should be in Bethlehem the next day.

Rather than being in a fever of anticipation as I was, Elimelech seemed almost to dread the coming interview. Sensing his mood, I kept quiet with great difficulty.

Neither of us slept much that night. After we had both tossed for a long time, Elimelech drew me into his arms and whispered, "Whatever comes, we are the Lord's people, and He will never forsake us. He always cares for His own." And clinging to that thought, he soon was asleep.

But as I lay there, instead of feeling secure in his words and comforted by his arms, I only felt confined and entrapped. I am sure that the Lord never forsakes us, I thought rebelliously, but it seems He has forgotten to do anything for our care. I would be ashamed to care for my children so!

As Elimelech left the next morning, he squeezed my shoulder and said, "Tonight we will talk."

How restless I was that day! And Mahlon and Chilion, sensing my mood, were also restless and quarrelsome. Finally I sent them to visit Cousin Leah. After a time of flitting from one thing to another, I forced myself to sit at the loom and work on a robe that I had started for Elimelech.

While I was preparing our evening meal, Elimelech came, but he was accompanied by our sons, so I knew that our conversation must wait until they were asleep.

At last the moment came, and we walked outside and up the stairs to sit on the roof under the brilliant stars in the cool of the evening. Elimelech was silent for some time and then spoke abruptly. "Abel brought back the report as I requested." His voice did not sound happy, and I felt a knot in my throat.

"The report was not good?" I asked.

"Oh, yes, the report was excellent. If Abel is to be believed, and I am sure that he is, the land of Moab is lush and green. The grapes are excellent this year. Barley and wheat harvest were both very good. And while the people do not actually welcome strangers, they do not repel them either. Others of our nation have moved to Moab, and they have not suffered harm."

"But that is wonderful! How can you sound so gloomy?"

"Oh, Naomi, I do not want to leave our homeland! I am not a bit sure that it would be right. But I do not want to see you and our sons suffer either."

My heart was stirred at his pain and indecision. "Surely we do not have to decide tonight," I said. "We could not easily move during this hot, dry season."

"And perhaps the Lord will send the rains this winter. Then we would not have to consider it at all." His voice sounded somewhat cheered.

"We could settle our minds that if the rains do not come, then we would go to Moab," I suggested. "That would give Yahweh a chance to stop our going if He does not want us to."

"Naomi, you studied the Law with your father, and I respected his wisdom and love for the Lord. Do you really think that it would be right for us to leave this land? Bethlehem is our 'place of blessing.'"

"If this is the place of blessing, what would a place of the curse be?" Sarcasm edged my voice. "Elimelech, we must be practical. Our fathers, Abraham, Isaac, and Jacob, all loved the Lord, and each of them left this land when it was practical."

"But, Naomi, they put themselves and their families in danger when they did," he reminded me urgently.

"Why did the Lord give us a mind if we were not to use it? Our responsibility is to care for our family the best we can. And after all, you are not one who worships heathen gods—one whom this famine was sent to judge."

"Perhaps you are right, but how would this move affect our sons? Would they not be drawn away from the true religion by associating with only heathen children?"

"How could they turn to false gods when you and I have taught them so carefully? Perchance we could even teach our heathen neighbors of the true God," I countered.

He sighed. "I pray that the rains will come."

But the rains did not come. The winter months dragged by, and the clouds that occasionally darkened the sky were barren.

Reluctantly Elimelech made plans to leave for Moab. We had told Mahlon and Chilion of the intended move, and already Elimelech spent extra time training them in the Law lest they be drawn away from the truth. "Remember, my sons, this famine has come from Yahweh because His people have turned aside to other gods. Our God will not share our worship. What does the Law say about this, Mahlon?"

And Mahlon promptly quoted from the commandments, "I am the Lord your God, who brought you out of the land of Egypt, out of the house of slavery. You shall have no other gods before Me. You shall not make for yourself an idol, or any likeness of what is in heaven above or on the earth beneath or in the water under the earth. You shall not worship them or serve them; for I, the Lord your God, am a jealous God."

Then it would be Chilion's turn, and he would quote some other portion from the Law for his worried father.

There was also the problem of the servants. Elimelech was adamant that only those servants who of their own choice wished to go to Moab should accompany us. And so he gathered the servants and spoke to them. "My family will be moving to Moab for a brief stay at the end of this winter. If any of you wish to go with us, you may, of course, but if you do not, you will be given your freedom. The decision is wholly your own."

The result was that only our sons' nurse, a woman devoted to the boys, decided to make the sojourn with us.

When Elimelech visited Cousin Leah to tell her of our plans, he came home visibly upset. "She absolutely refuses to go with us," he stated briefly.

Trying to hide my relief, I asked, "What will she do then?"

"I do not know," he answered heavily, and he walked out of the house.

Well, we cannot just leave her alone, I thought. Something will have to be done.

I went to visit Cousin Leah myself to see what could be done. When I broached the subject, she flared at me, "This is your doing! Elimelech would never choose to leave his land and his people!"

"Cousin Leah, be reasonable. This drought and the awful dust are hard on Mahlon and Chilion. And Elimelech is in danger of losing his flock. How can we just sit here and do nothing?"

"Your sons are far from starvation, and the flock is still large. You are just greedy and ambitious, Naomi. No good will come of this. You will see! And I certainly will not go along and be a part of your foolishness!"

"As you wish, Cousin Leah," I replied curtly, and I left her, determined to let Elimelech deal with her in the future.

The very next day Elimelech told me that his cousin Reuben had agreed to provide for Cousin Leah. "I will leave him a portion of our sheep to help him in caring for her," he added. "He has already lost most of his in caring for his own family, but he is willing to look after her."

And so we waited for the caravan that would provide our protection to Moab. Our destination was Kir-haraseth, unless something along the route particularly pleased Elimelech.

The caravan arrived at the appointed time, and we were in a flurry of activity making last-minute preparations.

Mahlon faced the journey with enthusiasm, but Chilion was silent, and I occasionally caught him looking very sad. None of our cheering words seemed to help although he pretended that all was well. "How like his father he is," I sighed.

Elimelech continued to worry over the sheep. It would be hard for them to keep up with the caravan, but we dare not travel by ourselves for fear of thieves or raiding bands of Midianites. Our herdsmen had agreed to help us take the flock to Moab before returning to Israel as free men.

But the sheep did keep up, and things got much easier after we crossed the Jordan, and there was grass for them to eat along the dusty road.

Even though the trip began as the most exhausting experience of my life, I was not discouraged. I kept my mind on Moab, lush and green, and envisioned our sheep grazing on the hills and our sons playing in the shade of the trees.

When we crossed the Jordan River, the trip became more pleasant. The road was still dusty and long, but the hills and valleys around began to be green. Chilion even began to look more cheerful. And Mahlon—how boisterous he was! He sang and shouted, running until he wore himself out. Then he would walk quietly or take a turn riding the donkey. But the gleam never left his eyes till they closed in sleep each night. Even Elimelech became less concerned.

After we reached the border of Moab, Elimelech watched the surrounding terrain closely and spoke with any Moabites that we encountered. But not until we reached Kir-haraseth did he decide to let the caravan go on without us. We camped on the outskirts of the city while he made inquiries. Already the sheep appeared to be in better flesh, and we were able to buy lovely, fresh fruits and vegetables in the market.

Then one evening Elimelech entered the tent with good news. "Tomorrow we will move to our home. It is less than a day's journey from Kir-haraseth. I have heard that other sons of Israel live there. Perhaps there the temptations will not be so great for our sons," he added.

"Do you think that we will find an empty house?" I asked.

"I fear that we will not, but we will build our own," he replied. "It will not be long either way until you are again living in a house of your own." His smile let me know that he understood my need to be keeping house properly.

That night Elimelech and I were both restless, and sleep did not come for a long time. I lay wondering, What will our new house be like? Will the people be friendly? Well, we will make do. It will only be for a year or two.

* * *

Now Naomi smiled at her false reckoning of the future that night 10 years ago. Just before she drifted off to sleep, she whispered God's words spoken to Joshua, "Be strong and courageous! Do not tremble or be dismayed, for the Lord your God is with you wherever you go."

"Thank You, Lord, for keeping Your promise," she murmured sleepily.

NAOMI AWOKE TO FIND RUTH KNEELING by her pallet, gently shaking her shoulder. "Are you rested for another day, my mother?" was Ruth's quiet greeting.

"Yes, and is all well with you?" She was careful not to ask, Are you sorry that you decided to come? Ruth's decision to accompany her mother-in-law was a precious bond between them. To doubt it now was to doubt the sincerity of Ruth's love for her and also to doubt Ruth's newfound faith in the God of Israel.

But Ruth answered Naomi's unspoken question as she replied, "I am so glad that I came with you! I have a peace within my heart that I have never before known. All is very well with me! I am even enjoying this journey—seeing things that I have never seen before—sleeping in a tent—it is all new and interesting to me."

Still chatting, the women quickly dressed, then folded their little tent before partaking of the dried fruit and parched grain that was their breakfast.

Soon the caravan was moving down the road. For a time Naomi was attentive to her surroundings, listening to the occasional birdsong on the morning air and eagerly watching for the tiny spring flowers that bloomed along the road. But as the morning slipped by, her thoughts drifted back to the time of her family's settling in Moab.

She remembered her delight in the new house that Elimelech had built for them on the outskirts of the village. Instead of building just one room, as most people did, Elimelech had built two rooms with the wall between enclosing the courtyard on the third side. In fact, that house was almost as nice as the one that they had left in Bethlehem, in spite of being smaller.

She remembered her joy in discovering that there were indeed two other Israelite families living in the same village.

But most deeply, she remembered the pain of the first real disillusionment of their stay in Moab. Strangely, it was not the Moabites who had caused her sorrow but the Israelites.

How thrilled we were to find two families of our people living nearby, Naomi remembered. When Elimelech told me, my first thought was that now our children could stick together and not be influenced by Moab and her people. All the time I busily settled into our new house, I made plans including these Israelite families who, I was sure, would be our dear friends and confidants in this strange land.

I was surprised when no one from the Israelite families came to welcome us to the village, but I assumed that they hesitated to bother us, knowing how busy we must be. Perhaps, they did not even know that we also were Israelites. I was sure that they had to be aware of our arrival. A new face in town always caused a lot of chatter, and word traveled as quickly as the sparrow's flight.

As soon as we were settled in, I set out to meet these two women, taking Mahlon and Chilion with me. I wondered why I had not met them already on trips to the village well.

It is not that the women of Moab have been unkind, I thought to myself as I hurried along. They have just ignored me. But it will be so good to have a friend who thinks and feels as I do!

"Do you think that is the right house?" I asked Mahlon doubtfully. "It seems to fit the description that your father gave me."

"Yes, I am sure that it is." Mahlon was always pleased to be referred to for advice.

The door of the house in question was open, and as we approached, I called, "May peace be upon this house."

There was a stir from the dimness within, and a woman some years older than myself appeared in the door-way. "Peace be upon you also," she replied automatically while looking at me questioningly.

"You are a woman of Israel, are you not?" I asked.

"Yes, I am Miriam, wife of Abidan. And you must be the wife of Elimelech. Won't you sit down?" Her manner had warmed somewhat, but she still seemed very reserved.

"Thank you. Yes, I am Naomi, and I have been so eager to know you and your family. Do you have children? I have brought my sons so that they could get acquainted with your children." I sat down in the courtyard and nudged my sons down beside me.

"My sons are out in the hills working with their father." Her tone of voice and look at my sons seemed to imply that my boys would do well to be out working too.

Defensively, I replied, "Our sons have never been strong enough for such strenuous work. We are hoping that living here will improve their health."

She just looked at me, so I rushed on, "We were wondering if you would like to have your sons study the Law with ours. Elimelech is an excellent teacher," I added.

She hesitated, and I thought she seemed embarrassed, but surely that was my imagination. Then she answered, "I doubt if our sons would have any time to study with your husband. They work every day, you see."

"Oh, but you must know how important it is that they learn the Law so that they do not stray away from the God of our fathers and His commandments." I was seated facing the open door of her house, and even as I spoke, my eye caught the gleam of something made of metal sitting on a shelf. My heart sank. I pulled my eyes away lest my staring should embarrass us both, but as I looked at my shamefaced hostess, I knew that my eyes had not deceived me. It was an idol.

Somehow I made my good-byes, even more eager to leave than I had been to meet this woman of Israel. Motioning to my sons to follow, I hurried down the street toward home. My thoughts were in a jumble of misery.

It was Mahlon's words that made me realize just how fast a pace I was setting. "Mother, you are hurrying so fast that we almost have to run to keep up. And besides, this is not the way to the other Israelite family's house. What is wrong?" This last was asked as he looked into my face.

His complaint brought me to a halt. "Oh, Mahlon, do you not understand? Those people worship heathen gods. They have not been true to the God of Israel. And I so much wanted you, my sons, to have friends of our own people!" I was near to tears, and my voice trembled.

Chilion spoke up then. "I saw that ugly little idol, too, Mother. But maybe the other Israelite family will worship our God."

"I did not like that woman much anyway," Mahlon added. "We probably would not like her sons either."

In spite of my sorrow, I smiled at their attempts to comfort me, but resolutely I refused to visit another strange house that day.

That evening as we told Elimelech our story, he did not seem nearly as shocked as I had expected. "Are you not horrified that this could be so?" I asked impatiently.

"I am hurt deep inside whenever I hear of any of our people turning aside from the Lord God, but I am not surprised. After all, the reason for the famine at home was the idolatry of our people. And a family who has left the Land of Promise is even more likely to have left their God also."

The pain in his voice was obvious, and it caused my own heart to ache anew. So I changed the subject, and we finished our meal in slightly better spirits.

Later that night, I prayed, "O God, keep my sons from evil in this strange land." But even as I voiced the words, I wondered if God heard me in this house in a village of Moab.

In the morning Elimelech noticed my troubled face.

"Today," he said, correctly guessing the cause of my consternation, "I will talk with Ochran, the other Israelite man in this village. You just leave this to me."

Relief filled my heart at his words. All through the day, I awaited his report with anxiety.

Perhaps I had never before realized the vast difference between ourselves and these people of Moab. Although their manner of dress and customs were not far removed from our own, and their language was very similar, knowing that they worshiped the awful god Chemosh left a wide gap between us.

How could I be friends with a woman who would allow her child to be offered as a human sacrifice? How could my sons grow up strong and pure among a people who committed immorality as a part of their worship?

It was that day that I began to doubt the wisdom of our move to Moab.

At supper that evening Elimelech guided the conversation away from the Israelite neighbors in Moab. He discussed the beauty of the hills, the birds, everything but what my anxious heart wanted to know. Deep inside, I knew that his evasiveness was my answer.

After the meal, he gave our sons their usual lesson in the Law, and then they were settled into bed for the night.

"Let us step outside and enjoy the evening," I said to Elimelech. Somehow he must talk to me of what he now knew. I dreaded to hear, but I must know.

But even after we were outside, he stood silent gazing at the beauty of the heavens.

"The family of Ochran also worship strange gods?" I finally asked, breaking the silence.

"Yes, Naomi, they do. They would be glad to be friends —if we do not preach at them. They are quite content with their life as it is." The sadness in his voice pained me, but I could not leave it alone.

"Then what are we to do? Whom do we associate with? What are Mahlon and Chilion to do for friends?"

"I have decided that Mahlon and Chilion shall go to the hills with me and help care for the sheep. I can teach them while we work, and it will keep them away from evil companions." He looked at me almost sternly. "I do not wish to discuss this further or to have an argument."

"Yes, Elimelech," I acquiesced, barely above a whisper.

And while I did not think my sons strong enough to work with the sheep, I could think of no better solution.

*　*　*

"But it was only a stopgap," Naomi now whispered. "Boys grow up, and our troubles were only beginning."

"O Lord, how we failed You in taking our sons to Moab. But I praise You for bringing good out of evil."

6

WITH EACH MILE TRAVELED, Naomi felt an inner burden lighten. She was going home. In her mind Bethlehem and happiness were intertwined, while memories of Moab seemed dark and dreary.

As she walked, Naomi's thoughts again journeyed into the past.

Each year in Moab, I assured myself that the problems would fade away, but each year the troubles multiplied. Word from home remained discouraging, and we stayed on in Moab.

When Elimelech first took our sons with him to care for the sheep, I longed to be out in the hills with them. But my place was in our house.

One of the first major setbacks that we experienced was a disease that hit our flocks. The sheep died by the score, and Elimelech's shoulders bowed in depression. This depression completely changed my husband, and because of his state, he slacked off in teaching our sons, and eventually he stopped altogether.

Even after our remaining sheep were healthy and flourishing, Elimelech remained discouraged. He became more and more withdrawn until eventually he ignored his sons and me completely. His only concern seemed to be for the sheep; they became an obsession with him.

These changes did not occur all at once. But in the course of seven years, Elimelech changed from a warm, thoughtful man into a sullen recluse.

At first I tried to reason with him. I reminded him of Job and all that he had suffered. "And yet he did not turn his face to the wall and sulk. He did not understand the sufferings that God allowed to come into his life, but he continually sought God's answer, and finally he found it. And then the Lord blessed Job with twice what he had before. Oh, Elimelech, if you hate it so here, then let us go back to Bethlehem. But please be yourself again!"

My reprimand did stir Elimelech to speech, but I found his answer very disquieting. "We cannot go back! The drought is still heavy on the land of Israel, and the sheep would die if we took them back to that very short pasture! Do you not understand? We must stay here until the drought is over!" His eyes and voice were full of desperate fury.

Another time I approached the subject from another angle. "Elimelech, why do you not teach our sons the Law? You have not quoted to them from the Scripture for months." As he looked at me in grim silence, I continued, "I am sure that it would help you also. If you do not teach them, who will?"

His patience and silence ended abruptly as he grasped my shoulders and shook me. "You teach them!" he fairly screamed. "You always know everything and have all the answers. Just leave me alone."

He stalked out of our house and did not return that day or even at night. I could not sleep when I finally lay down upon my mat. Where is he? Will he be all right? Will he ever again be the man I once knew?

Gradually I began to turn to the God of my father. Even as I tried to pray, words and thoughts came unbidden to my mind. "You are out of the place of blessing. Why should you expect God to solve your problems? You wanted your own way, and you got it. Now you must bear the consequences!"

But though the heavens seemed as brass, I continued to pray.

My sons knew my heart was heavy, and I am sure that they also sorrowed over the change in their father. Their attitude toward me fluctuated between loving concern and angry disdain.

I did not try to teach them the Scriptures because I knew they would properly resent being taught by a woman. But when they began to assert their independence and spend time with young men of Moab, as well as with the sons of Abidan and Ochran, I rebuked them and urged them to have no communication with the ungodly.

I remember the scorn in Mahlon's voice as he said, "And who should we be with, Mother? Our godly father who never speaks, or our righteous mother who drove him to this condition? No, Mother, you cannot rule our lives as you have our father's!"

"That is not just!" I cried as Mahlon slammed out of the house. Chilion hesitated, then followed his brother.

As I wept that day, I realized that part of what Mahlon had said was true. While I was not totally responsible for Elimelech's state, I had urged him to leave Bethlehem. And I was sure that that was the root of his problem.

My sons spent more and more time with the youths of Moab. As I lay upon my pallet at night, I imagined the terrible places they might be. And on special festival days in honor of the god Chemosh, my heart was heavy. Were they taking part in the worship of that awful god? I knew that sexual immorality was a part of that worship, and I feared lest my sons fall before the temptation. "O Lord, do not let it be!"

Frequently, when they finally returned home, it was with reeling steps and drunken laughter.

Day and night my heart ached. Each day I worked as though there would be no other, trying to forget the pain.

"O Lord," I cried night after night, "You must help me. I can bear no more!"

By day I comforted myself, "Things must get better. They can be no worse. Elimelech will get well. My sons will listen to him. The drought will end in Israel, and we will go home. All will be well again. After all, we are Israelites. We have never bowed to foreign Gods—at least I know that Elimelech and I have not," I added truthfully.

But things did get worse. Elimelech became sick. It did not start as a serious illness. I had seen him often declare such a slight fever to be nothing, and he would go out to care for his sheep. But this time was different. Immediately he took to his bed. He refused to eat, only accepting water to drink. For hours he lay on his mat, face to the wall. My attempts to nurse him only made him angry.

One morning Mahlon drew me outside the house so that his father would not overhear. "Mother, what are we going to do? He will die if he does not eat soon!"

"I do not know," I admitted. "I have no answers or suggestions this time."

But I did feel a gentle pricking in my heart. Words of my father, of Elimelech, and even of Cousin Leah marched through my mind, and the scriptures that I had memorized accompanied them. That afternoon while Mahlon cared for the sheep, and Chilion sat with his father, I slipped off by myself.

"O God," I cried, "I have sinned. I thought I could handle things myself. I thought my reasoning was better than Your Law. Lord, will You forgive me? If I could, I would offer a ram for my transgression, but I am far from Shiloh.

Would You accept my broken heart as an offering and forgive my sins?

"And, Lord, You know the mess that things are in because of my sin. You know that my sons are far from You, and my husband is as one dead even though he is yet living. O my God, would You give Elimelech peace and bring my sons to Yourself?"

This time as I prayed, the heavens were not as brass. I knew that it was my proud heart that had kept my prayers from being answered. I headed home that afternoon with a quiet peace within. God was in control.

Even finding Elimelech's condition worsened on my return could not extinguish the hope within my heart.

Mahlon had also returned, and he, Chilion, and I sat vigil by Elimelech's pallet. As evening drew on, his fever raised, and he began muttering and then cried aloud in his delirium. Often his words were unintelligible to us, but we caught an occasional word, "Shiloh." "Father." "Lamb."

Mahlon tried to reassure him that the lambs were all right, but the sheep did not seem to be his chief concern. He continued his rambling, fluctuating between low mutterings and shouts. But gradually the fever eased, and his voice grew still.

Mahlon and Chilion crept off to their own mats to rest, but I continued sitting by my husband, my hand resting on his arm.

Then I, too, must have slept, for I roused with a start to see Elimelech looking at me. His gaze was warm, clear eyed, and aware for the first time in many months.

"Naomi," he whispered. I leaned close to hear him. He reached for my hand, and I clasped his hand in mine. "Naomi, I have much to say and little time, so listen closely."

As I would have spoken, he placed a shaking finger against my lips. "No," he insisted weakly, "just listen."

"I have sinned against you, my love, first, by bringing

you to this land, and then by blaming you for my own weakness."

Again I would have spoken, and again he stopped me.

"You need a strong husband, and I have been weak. I am asking you to forgive me."

I could only nod while tears streamed down my face.

"Ah, good," he breathed. "Somehow I knew you would." With a trembling hand he attempted to wipe the tears from my cheeks. "I have asked the Lord God to forgive my weakness and pride, and I know that He has. I long to offer a trespass offering, but I will not return to Shiloh. Naomi, when you return to our homeland, you must go to Shiloh and offer a burnt offering for me. Yahweh knows that my heart is now surrendered to Him, but I want you to let people know that when I died, I was back in right standing with my God."

"I will, Elimelech, I will, but you must get well, and we will go to Shiloh together. I also will offer the sacrifice for myself. I, also, have surrendered my will to Jehovah. I have been self-willed and proud. I ask that you forgive me, also, my lord." The title of respect was new to my lips.

I could see that Elimelech noticed, and delight was in his eyes. "Oh, my love, why did we wait so long? But now you must call our sons. I must speak to them while I still can."

I went to call Mahlon and Chilion, knowing that Elimelech was growing steadily weaker. They roused quickly at my touch and hurried to their father's side. Quietly, I cautioned them, "He would speak to you, and his strength is waning. If you let him speak without interruption, then he can rest again."

They nodded their understanding and knelt to hear him better. "We are here, Father," Mahlon said. Chilion reached out and laid his hand gently on this father's wasted shoulder.

"My sons," and Elimelech's eyes were full of love and pride as he gazed at them. "I have failed you, my sons. I brought you to a strange land; I did not faithfully teach you the commandments of our God. I now ask you to forgive me."

He paused and looked at them beseechingly.

Chilion's voice trembled, "Of course, Father."

Mahlon's "Yes, Father" was spoken at the same moment.

"And, my sons, I ask you to take your mother back to Bethlehem, the 'place of blessing.'"

I knew that only sheer determination kept Elimelech alert. At their assent to his request, the tension left his body. "It is well," he whispered, and his eyes closed. He drifted off into a deep sleep.

Before the sun rose to light the new day, his soul had left the weary body.

"O my God," I whispered, when I realized that my dear husband had been gathered to his Father, "thank You for Your goodness to us. Thank You for answering my prayer and giving Elimelech peace. And thank You that we will be going home soon."

I arose to tell my sons that their father was gone. Then together we set about the sad duties of the day. My aching heart found no release in tears. The only surcease I found was in constant activity.

The other Israelite families were notified, and they hurried to join us, but their words were of no comfort to me. They had no peace themselves and could only wail at this dreadful calamity.

"Shall I hire mourners?" Mahlon asked me.

"No," I replied. "Your father needs no hired Moabite wailers. Now he is at peace and gathered to his own people. It would be a mockery to hear the wailing of strangers."

I was thankful for the many demands of the day. There

was no time to really mourn or to realize my new state as a widow.

But the day ended, and the quiet night settled down. There was no one needing my attention and nothing that I needed to do. The spot beside my mat, where Elimelech had lain, now was starkly empty. Sobs shook my body and tore at my throat. All the hurt of the last seven years seemed to erupt from my aching heart.

At last the storm of grief was spent, and I drifted off into sleep, still aware of my great loss, and yet comforted by my renewed faith in the God of my fathers. Although I was now no man's wife, I was a child of the God of all the earth.

* * *

Naomi came back to the present realizing that tears were coursing down her cheeks. It is a wonder that the fountain of my tears still flows, she thought, wiping her face. It should have run dry long before this.

And yet though the troubles and pain have been frequent, I have not lost my peace or trust in my God.

"I thank You, Lord God, that You have never failed me. Thank You that Elimelech and I had those moments of reconciliation before his death. And I thank You that though my life has been hard, You have been teaching me to trust You more."

7

THE DAYS HAD PASSED, but Mahlon and Chilion seemed to be making no preparations for the move. Finally, one day I broached the subject while we sat around our evening meal.

"Are you planning to go back to Bethlehem before the summer comes, my sons? I need to make the necessary preparations," I added hastily, seeing the quick anger in Mahlon's eyes.

He delayed answering, but when he did his answer was clear. "No, Mother, we cannot go yet. The drought is still on in Israel. There would be no grass for the sheep."

"But you . . ." My sentence was hardly begun before Mahlon impatiently interrupted.

"Yes, I know that I promised Father that I would take you back. And I will, but not yet! We have to be reasonable!" His tone implied that I was not, and I swallowed my own reasoning and objections.

Chilion sat eating as if food were the only concern that he felt. Clearly he was not going to enter the argument.

Since Elimelech's death, Mahlon was the head of the house. All decisions must be made by Mahlon and Chilion, with Mahlon as the elder having the final say. My only recourse was to submit and leave these matters in their hands.

But my heartache was almost unbearable as I lay on my lonely mat that night. "O God," I cried, "You know how I want to go back—and now I cannot! What am I to do? You know that I would set out alone, but my sons would never allow it, and it would bring shame upon them if I would." My tears flowed freely that night as I poured out my sorrow and frustration to the Lord.

Then gradually my thoughts quieted, and my tears ceased. A gentle thought entered my consciousness. God had demanded submission of me, not a trip to Bethlehem. I must practice that submission and leave the rest to Him. Peace crept into my heart again as I yielded my son's decision to God. "Lord, in Your time," I whispered. "Take me home in Your time."

In the days ahead I found that decision tried frequently, and I was not always sweetly yielding. Habits of many years were hard to break. I cried out to God in my frustration.

At first, after their father's death, my sons spent their time either in the hills with the sheep or at home with me. But as the months passed, they began to seek the pleasures of Moab. When I realized the pull that Moab had upon them, my heart trembled in fear. Were they falling into the worship of the Moabite god Chemosh or the immorality that was so much a part of life here in Moab? My old fears returned, and a new one was added to the list. What if they should want to marry girls from Moab?

"Lord, will You not end the drought in Israel so that we can go home?" I pleaded. "My sons will not go while the drought remains. And, Lord, they must get away from here—they must!"

The temptation was great to take matters into my own hands. One day I casually remarked to Mahlon, "I wish we were back in Bethlehem so that we could arrange your marriage."

Mahlon's reply was abrupt, "What father would betroth his daughter to a man with a pitiful flock of starving sheep?"

"O Lord, I have said the wrong thing again," I breathed. And I carefully avoided the subject of brides in the future.

I feared that my sons would be thinking of brides themselves. After all, they were both of the age to be married. And if we did not go back to Bethlehem, only Moabite girls remained. True, there were the daughters in the two Israelite families living in the village, but one daughter had already married a Moabite, and the other girls were not what my sons should have for wives. They did not keep the Law or serve our own true God. My sons' marrying pagan Israelite girls would be little improvement over their marrying pagan Moabites.

Night after night I lay agonizing in prayer. My worries plagued me as I went about my work through the day. I bombarded heaven with my requests as I continually called upon the Lord God.

Then the blow fell. It was morning and we sat in the courtyard eating our simple meal. I sensed that something was different. Neither of my sons seemed in the usual hurry to leave for the hills and flocks. Mahlon was grimly determined about something, and Chilion was definitely nervous.

Tension was thick in the air. I forced myself to swallow bits of food while I waited for one of them to speak.

I looked up at Mahlon and caught his gaze on me. Our glances locked, and we both smiled almost against our will. We are so much alike, I thought, both grimly preparing for battle and dreading the pain that we know it will bring. And I do not even know the battlefield, I only recognize the signs of war.

Even as these thoughts flashed through my mind, Mahlon began to speak. "Mother, I have found the girl that I want for my wife, and Chilion has also."

"And where," I asked icily, "have you met these girls?"

Still Chilion did not look up, and I turned again to Mahlon. "Who are these girls that you want as your wives?" I struggled to keep my voice even.

"Mother, I will be glad to tell you about Ruth and Orpah and where they live. Ruth is the daughter of Arod who lives in the large stone house by the well. She is a lovely girl and will be good company for you as well as being the right wife for me."

Numbly I turned to Chilion, "And the girl you want to marry—who is she?"

When he finally spoke, his voice was enthusiastic. "Oh, Mother, you will like her!" I could see that he had made his decision himself and not been led along by Mahlon. "She is so pretty!" he continued. "And she is sweet and gentle too. Her name is Orpah, and she lives with her brother Deuel. Her father is dead."

"And she is a Moabite—both of them are Moabites!" I broke in. My voice began to rise as my control slipped. "How could you? You know you must not marry Moabites. Do you plan to become children of Chemosh? Will you offer my grandchildren to him?"

"Stop!" Mahlon's voice slashed across my rising hysteria. "We plan to marry these girls. You will go to their homes and make marriage arrangements. This is your responsibility since our father is dead. You will accept our wives as your respected daughters. Is that clear?"

Gasping, I ran from the courtyard. As I fled, bitterness welled up within me. "O God, have You heard my prayers at all? How can You let my sons do this? I cannot make marriage agreements for pagan brides for my sons!"

On I ran until at last I collapsed on a grassy hillside and let the floods of grief sweep over me. Time passed unnoticed as I fought the battle of pain and rage. Yes, the rage against the Lord God. I knew that He was in control. And yet He had allowed this to happen. Had I not suffered enough? Admittedly, I had been willful and proud, and even ambitious, but I had repented and turned back to the Lord. I had lost my husband. I had no way of returning to Israel in spite of my desires. And I had prayed day and night to the Lord God of Israel for my sons. And now this!

The sun was low in the west when the storm of emotion began to abate, leaving me exhausted. In the calm of that moment, the voice of God seemed to speak quietly, "Naomi, you are My beloved child. Will you trust Me and submit to Me in this very difficult test? Will you trust your sons to Me? Will you let Me deal with them and teach them My ways? And will you take these heathen girls and love them as the daughters that you have always wanted? Will you teach them by your life and by the Scriptures about Me?"

My spirits lifted a little. Could I do that? I had always planned to share my faith and my God with these heathen Moabites, but aside from quoting portions from the Law to my servant girls each morning, my efforts at proselytizing had been few.

I could hardly believe the stirrings of hope within my heart. By God's grace I would accept the inevitable and do my best to show these girls the benefit of serving the God of Israel.

I arose from the grass and walked almost briskly home, my mind filled with my good intentions and plans.

*   *   *

Naomi smiled contentedly in the darkness. "O my Father, how I thank You that You broke through my bitterness and pain to show me the flicker of hope that brightened those troubled days. And, Lord, You gave me Ruth—how can I ever thank You for that!"

8

RUTH WATCHED HER MOTHER-IN-LAW anxiously
the next morning. She knew that Naomi had been
near the breaking point. But Naomi caught her
searching gaze and gave her a bright smile.

"Isn't it a lovely day! I feel so refreshed this morning."
Ruth's worried face relaxed into an answering smile.

"You look well this morning, my mother. You must
have slept well," but there was a question in her tone.

"Oh, I was awake some as usual, but I have been remembering God's wonderful blessings to me."

"Blessings?" Ruth's voice was incredulous.

"Yes, blessings, Ruth, and you are one of His greatest
gifts of blessing." Naomi gave the puzzled girl a hug, and
they hurried on with the morning's ritual of packing up
and preparing for the day's journey.

Tonight camp would be made at the Jordan River so
that the crossing could start early in the morning. And tomorrow she would be in Israel! Although it would be the
third day before the caravan reached Bethlehem, the thought
of being so close to Israel quickened Naomi's heart.

Naomi's step was sprightly that morning and her thoughts cheerful. Is it not amazing, she thought, that the act of obedience changes the dreaded step into a thing of joy? In spite of my submission to my sons' will in the choosing of their brides, how I dreaded making the arrangements and meeting their parents! My pride made it so difficult for me to ask heathen Moabites for their daughters as wives for my sons. And of course, I still did not think that my boys were taking a proper step. But I would leave that to the Lord.

That evening when I had returned from my own personal battleground in the hills, I found Mahlon pacing our courtyard. "Mother," he nearly shouted, "where have you been? I have been anxious, but I did not know where to look for you!"

"I am sorry, Son. I needed to be alone, and time slipped away from me. Where is Chilion? I wish to speak with both of you."

Mahlon eyed me warily, uneasy at my calmness. "He should be here soon," he replied.

"Then I will see to the meal, and we can talk afterward."

When Chilion came from the flocks, we ate a rather silent meal. When the servants had cleared away the remains, I spoke. "My sons," and my nails bit into my hands as I gripped them together, but my voice remained steady. "Mahlon, Chilion, I was wrong to shout at you in anger. I still believe that it is not right for you to marry any but godly Israelite girls. But you are men now, and I will abide by your decision. You must now tell me what to do to secure your brides. Are the customs here the same as in Israel?"

As I spoke, I watched my sons' expressions pass from uneasiness to shock and then to smiles of relief. Mahlon's "Thank you, Mother" was hearty, and he clasped my hand, while Chilion gave me his quiet smile.

We spent some time discussing the gifts that they would present the brides and their families. Then we went on to plan changes necessary in our house to accommodate the new couples. A third room would be built, replacing the wall at the end of the courtyard. The marriages would not take place until the third room was finished.

When we finally retired to our mats, my head was full of plans, and my heart was full of praise at God's mercy in softening my heart to do His bidding. I still did not understand this situation, but I would yield and accept, leaving the results to Him. And in this acceptance I was at peace.

My peace was threatened, however, when the hour approached for the visits to the houses of Ruth's and Orpah's families. Servants had been sent to both houses to prepare the families for my visit, and in spite of my quaking heart, I set out.

"Peace be on you," I greeted Ruth's father as I bowed low.

"And on you peace," he returned politely, also bowing.

Ruth's father seemed loud and uncouth, and my heart beat painfully as I thought what his daughter must be. But I was pleasantly surprised when she appeared in the courtyard. A slender girl with dark hair, her most arresting feature was her eyes. She was attractive but not really beautiful, until she smiled shyly. Then her whole face lit up, and I glimpsed a bit of the warm personality that had attracted my elder son.

I wondered if she had dreaded this meeting as much as I had. After the greetings, her father's bluster quieted, and our dealings were amicable.

Feeling somewhat better, I walked on to the house of Orpah's family. As her father was dead, I would deal with her mother and older brother. They were very poor.

Again the greetings were cordial. As we began our business, I noticed her brother's eyes glittering with greed. But the gifts agreed upon by my sons were acceptable with him.

They were generous by any standards, and would bring this family a sense of near wealth.

When our business was finished, I still had not caught a glimpse of the future bride. At last I asked the mother, "May I meet Orpah?"

Looking startled at my request, she left the courtyard, murmuring that she would see if Orpah were nearby.

I could see no reason why my request was out of the way. Is she deformed? or ill? Why this hesitation? Even as these thoughts flew through my mind, I realized how foolish they were. Chilion would never have chosen a defective bride. But still I wondered and worried as the moments passed.

Finally, the mother reappeared in the doorway of the house, and by the hand she led the reluctant Orpah. I realized how little Orpah wished for this meeting by the fact of her being in the house on a lovely day such as this. Indeed she had evidently been hiding from me.

Now she approached with her head bowed, and only after I spoke to her did she lift her eyes. While Ruth had been shy, this girl showed every sign of being terrified. But her fear could not detract from her beauty. She was fair skinned, and her features were delicate and perfectly shaped. I almost gasped in astonishment. So much for my fears of deformity!

Gently I tried to draw her out, but only when Chilion's name was mentioned did a tiny smile flit across her face.

As I left that house and started for my own, I smiled wryly. I realized these girls feared a foreign mother-in-law as much as I objected to heathen daughters-in-law! I had pictured them as being proud and hard, but they were only frightened girls. Surely I could win them over to myself— and then perhaps to the one true God.

The formal betrothal ceremonies soon took place, and work began on the addition to our house. With every brick laid, our residence here seemed more permanent. "But we are not here to stay!" I breathed to myself. "We must go back. O Lord, when will I go home? How much longer must I wait?" I kept my silence, however, knowing that any mention of the subject would cause strife.

The Lord gave me peace in spite of my longings. In fact, I enjoyed preparing for the two lovely girls who would become my daughters. I did my best to make their living quarters attractive and homey. While doing this work of love, I planned how I would show these girls my love and teach them of my God. During those hours it seemed impossible that my plans should fail.

The days flew by, and my eager sons brought home their brides. The wedding feast was not as elaborate as my own had been. But it was gay and noisy! I was thankful when it was over, the strangers were gone to their own houses, and quiet once again reigned.

Now began my opportunity to win my daughters-in-law. But somehow, things did not work out just as I had hoped. Perhaps if there had been only one addition to our family, things would have been different. I do not know. But Ruth and Orpah clung to one another and seemed to have no need of my companionship or advice. Both girls treated me with polite respect, and Orpah's respect was tinged with fear, I was sure.

Ruth and Orpah submitted quietly to listening to the Law as I quoted portions to all the women and girls in the house each morning. But neither ever asked a question, even when I asked them if they understood the words of the Scripture.

One morning after Scripture and prayers, I broke our normal routine. "Orpah, Ruth, would you come out for a walk with me? I would like to show you a favorite spot of mine." I smiled brightly, and both returned my smile but a bit uneasily.

As we walked, I told them how I had always loved to

be out in the hills as a girl. Ruth responded by remarking that she, too, preferred working out in the open.

I was delighted at this first real communication between us. I tried to include Orpah, but she remained quiet.

We came to "my" spot, a lovely shaded glen by the brook. The only noises there were the twittering of the birds and the cheerful gurgling and splashing of the water. We sat drinking in the fresh beauty, and I gained courage to begin.

"My daughters, Mahlon and Chilion may have told you that at first I objected to your marriages." Their quick glances at one another assured me that this was indeed the case. "I want you to know that the only reason that I objected was that our Law forbids such alliances. Just before our people came into the land of Canaan to live among heathen nations, the Lord God told us, 'You shall not intermarry with them; you shall not give your daughters to their sons, nor shall you take their daughters for your sons. For they will turn your sons away from following Me to serve other gods; then the anger of the Lord will be kindled against you, and He will quickly destroy you.'

"It was for this reason only that I objected. I have never heard anything but good of either of you, and now I see that you are daughters to be proud of.

"I love my sons dearly, but I have always sorrowed that I had no daughters to share in the things that I enjoy. I want you to be my dearly loved daughters, not just the wives of my sons."

I paused a moment to steady my voice before continuing, "When I married, my husband's mother was long since gone to her fathers, but his old cousin was concerned about my being a proper wife. I resented her nosiness and bossiness, never realizing till much later that she really only wanted to help."

Tears filled my eyes, and I fought for control in order to continue. "I do not want that to happen between us."

I could not continue. The tears were rolling down my cheeks, and I bit my lip to stifle my sobs.

Ruth's arm was suddenly around my shoulders, and her voice was gentle. "Mother, we did not understand. We knew that you did not approve our husbands' choices, and we were sure that you were ashamed of us. We do not hate you," and she gave me a gentle squeeze, "but we do not understand many of your ways. Can you be patient with us as we learn?"

In answer I turned and gathered her into a warm embrace. Then I held out an arm to Orpah who joined us.

I was embarrassed by my emotion, yet I felt that the wall between us was partially broken down—at least with Ruth.

As we walked home that day, I determined to start anew in my quoting the Scripture each morning. Instead of teaching the Moabites the Law, I would begin right at the start with the account of the creation of the world. And I would go on to the history of our people, leaving the laws and rules until I came to them in the sequence of the Scripture.

I carried through with my plan, and I found Ruth and Orpah much more interested in the stories of history than they had been in the rules of our life.

That first morning after I had recited the account of creation, Ruth volunteered, "Our storytellers have a very similar account of the beginning of the world."

"Oh? Yes, I suppose they would since Lot would have known the story well. I wonder how much more we will find that we share in common?" was my reply.

Even the servants who shared our scripture time seemed eager to hear more, and I marveled that I had not thought to start with the stories of Genesis before.

Several days later, when we reached the story of Noah and the flood, we again found a similarity with the Moabite account.

But it was the story of Lot that elicited the most interest from Ruth and Orpah. It was a few days later that we started the story of Abraham and Lot, and I quoted as closely as possible from the words of Moses found in the Scripture. I had told the group of Moabites around me, my daughters-in-law and the servant girls, that Lot was their ancestor, so their attention was caught immediately.

There was little comment as I told of Abraham and Lot dividing the land, although several faces, including Ruth's, showed their disapproval of Lot's greed.

But the destruction of Sodom and Gomorrah made quite an impression. And the scheme of Lot's daughters to produce heirs left even these heathen girls aghast. The entire group was twittering like angry sparrows. I held up my hand, and they immediately became quiet. "Just a few more lines," I assured them, "and then we will discuss the story.

"And the first-born bore a son, and called his name Moab; he is the father of the Moabites to this day."

Again their faces showed shock, and I think few even listened as I continued, "And as for the younger, she also bore a son, and called his name Ben-ammi; he is the father of the sons of Ammon to this day."

Silence reigned for a moment after I had concluded, and then several voices spoke at once. Then the others desisted and let Ruth speak for them. "You mean that we are descended from Lot and his elder daughter?" Her voice still expressed disbelief. "Is that why your people treat us with scorn?"

"Yes, that is your ancestry, but no, that is not the trouble between Israelites and Moabites. That comes further along in the writings of Moses."

"But what else were those girls to do?" asked one of the servants. "They had no chance of a normal marriage!"

While we sat and discussed the story, I rejoiced that the wall was crumbling. We could now openly communicate. I glanced over at Orpah. She remained silent, but her eyes were bright and questioning, and she was certainly taking it all in. My heart warmed anew to this shy little daughter.

As I continued on through the Scriptures day by day, we shared together the excitement of the release of God's people from Egypt and His care of them in the wilderness. I told them of the hardships that the Israelites faced and the victories and defeats that they had experienced.

Then I told them how the king of Moab had wanted Baalam to curse Israel for him, but Baalam would not. But Israel had suffered because of Moab anyway. Twenty-four thousand Israelites had died because they had taken Moabite women and had joined in Moabite sacrifices and worship.

"But why should they blame us? Surely it was their own decision?" someone asked.

"Yes, that is true. But it is generally believed that although Baalam would not curse Israel for the king of Moab, he did provide him with a scheme to achieve his ends. He suggested that the Moabite women entice the men of Israel and then draw them into the worship of Baal of Peor. He knew that God would judge His people, and that many would be destroyed. Thus they would be weakened and be no threat to Moab.

"Scripture says, 'Then the Lord spoke to Moses, saying, "Be hostile to the Midianites and strike them; for they have been hostile to you with their tricks, with which they have deceived you in the affair of Peor."'

"You see, Baalam, who devised the scheme, was a Midianite."

The Moabites around me discussed this freely, some still feeling that Israel was excusing their own mistakes at the expense of others. But Ruth spoke up in defense of Israel. "I can see that it was a wicked trick, and Israel has the right to be angry with those involved. But just how do Israelites feel about Moabites today?" She turned to me with her question.

"Israelites are like all other peoples in one way," I replied. "No two of them feel exactly the same about anything. But most Israelites do not hate Moabites to the point of wishing to do them injury. I think most of my people just feel distrustful of the people of Moab, particularly their women."

The women and girls laughed, and they were seemingly satisfied with my answer, for the subject was dropped.

We had now reached the account of God's laws for His people, but the lists of rules were interspersed with stories of their wilderness adventures. And the Moabites saw the Law from a new perspective. While they still did not understand it all, they listened with more interest.

*   *   *

Naomi smiled now as she looked back on those happy days. That talk in the hillside retreat had been the beginning of their becoming a family.

"Thank You, Lord, for helping me to humble myself and to be honest with Ruth and Orpah. Thank You for the understanding You gave us. And Lord, bless my daughter Ruth, and help Orpah back in her old home. May she remember the Scriptures and be guided by them."

9

*A*S EVENING FELL, the caravan camped on the east bank of the Jordan River. Naomi hurried through her share of the evening chores and then drew apart to stand gazing off into the sunset. Home! Just across the river was Israel! How her heart leapt at the thought! Memories of her own land flooded through her. It had been 10 years, and yet it seemed as yesterday that she had walked those familiar trails.

Naomi looked around and saw Ruth standing not far away. Joining her daughter-in-law, she asked, "Do you feel afraid, my dear?"

Ruth's smile was warm as she answered, "Yes, I feel afraid and, also, brave. I am eager, and yet I long to hold back. Do you understand, my mother? I am not sure that I do!" And she laughed gaily at her own mixed emotions.

Naomi laid her arm around Ruth's shoulders and answered gently, "I certainly do understand as I have myself often experienced such confusion. You are a brave girl, Ruth, and the Lord will reward you for following Him."

Night was settling in as the two women walked quietly toward their little tent. Neither knew what the future held, but each was trusting the same One to prepare her way.

They discussed the rest of the trip a little longer, but Naomi was so worn from the day's trek that she drifted off to sleep.

Much later Naomi woke with a start at the wild scream of a lion. She lay utterly still until he screamed again, and she realized what it was that had awakened her.

Eventually the lion either moved on or went to sleep, and Naomi relaxed. Her thoughts journeyed back a few months. The events were all too fresh in her mind.

Those idyllic days of getting acquainted with my daughters-in-law came to a halt when the pestilence hit the village. The first I had heard of the sickness was on a cold, rainy morning in winter. Ruth and Orpah had been to the well that morning, and their steps were hurried as they entered the house and set down the heavy jars. I glanced up from my weaving and I felt uneasy as I saw their faces.

"What is it? What is wrong?"

"Oh, Mother, there is a terrible plague in the village. We heard of five sick people, and one old grandmother has died," Ruth's voice trembled.

"Are your parents and families well?"

"We did not hear otherwise, but we would like to go make sure—if we may?" While Ruth's voice was shaky, she did not look nearly so distraught as Orpah. Her face was pale.

"Orpah, do you have reason to think that someone who is dear to you is sick?" I held her twisting hands in mine.

"No," her voice was barely above a whisper, "I am just afraid. I do not know why, but I feel so afraid!" As soon as I released her hands, they were twisting in anguish again.

I patted her shoulder and squeezed Ruth's hand as I urged them out the door. "Go quickly and see that your families are well, and then come back and let me know also."

When they returned sometime later, their news was mostly good. None who lived at their parents' houses had fallen to the plague, but two more people in the village had died. And by the time they returned, our own home was affected. One of the little maidservants was gravely ill.

I was thankful for the little bit of nursing skill that I had learned in caring for my small sons years before as I cared for this desperately ill child. But my hours of care were of no avail, and before the next morning, she was dead.

So began our nightmare. First one and then another of our servants and neighbors sickened and died. Ruth quietly began to care for the ill ones of our household with me. Orpah took on the extra work of caring for the house and preparing meals.

I watched Orpah with concern. Her hands trembled, and tears rolled down her cheeks at the least provocation.

"Orpah," I insisted, "you must get more rest. We do not want you to sicken."

For the first time Orpah turned to me and clung tightly as I held her. "Oh, Mother, I am so afraid! It is not the work; I am not tired. But I am afraid, so afraid!" And as she clung, she wept piteously.

I did my best to comfort her, but her fears were so unspecific that I did not know what to say to help her.

Gradually she regained control, and I persuaded her to lie down in the quietness of an empty room.

Ruth and I were also feeling the strain. In spite of everything we did, sooner or later each one who sickened died.

Then just a few evenings later, Chilion staggered in with fever-flushed face and glazed eyes. My heart almost stopped. Then I began the automatic routine of getting the sick one to bed for the hours of careful tending.

Amazingly, now that the dreaded foe had struck her own husband, Orpah developed an almost passive calm. For hours she sat at Chilion's side, holding his hand, smoothing his blanket, or wiping his fevered brow with damp cloths.

Chilion had brief intervals of lucidity, but much of the time he was delirious. It was often difficult to tell his state of understanding.

One time he said, "Mother, I want to go back to Bethlehem. I do not like it here."

"Yes, my son, we will go back," I soothed.

"But Father said that we must wait," he objected.

In spite of myself, tears spilled from my eyes, and I choked back sobs to answer determinedly, "We will go back!"

Then Chilion was again fighting unseen enemies, and it took Orpah's and my combined strength to keep him on his mat.

Sometime later he again spoke to me. "Mother, sing me Moses' song of deliverance," he begged.

So I began shakily to sing that song of praise. As I repeated the words, "The Lord is my strength and song, And He has become my salvation; This is my God, and I will praise Him; My father's God, and I will extol Him." Chilion tried to sing with me, and my heart nearly broke at that breathy, wasted voice singing praise to the Lord God of Israel. He only sang a few lines before lapsing again into unconsciousness, but my heart clung to the reassurance that he had not forgotten his God.

Chilion's strength waned as the sickness progressed, and before the day was gone, his life was over.

When Orpah realized that he was dead, she did not become hysterical as I had expected, but rather, that frightful calm continued. It seemed that she had spent all her tears before the disaster struck, and now there were no more.

I felt ready to collapse but held on to my control by thinking of all the things that I must now be doing to help others.

Together we went to find Ruth. My control did snap when we discovered her kneeling by Mahlon, as he lay fighting for his life.

Orpah, upon seeing this brother ill also, wrenched away from my comforting arm and fled.

My own reaction amazed me. I was filled with anger, so enraged, in fact, that I lashed out at Ruth. "Why did you not call me? Have I no right to know that my eldest son lies dying?"

I would have continued, but the shocked expression on Ruth's face stopped me cold. "I did not call you, Mother, because you were busy with Chilion." Her quiet answer was given in calm dignity and served to rebuke my own temper. "Is Chilion . . . ?" She paused, not knowing how to ask, but I nodded wearily, knowing well enough what she meant.

"Yes, he is gone. How long has Mahlon been like this?"

I knelt with her beside his mat and touched his forehead as she answered, "He came in with a bad headache at midday. He has not seemed to be as bad as many of the others. Perhaps he will recover. You could pray to the Lord God of Israel that his life be spared." She looked at me hopefully, and my heart ached anew for her pain.

"Oh, Ruth," I answered her honestly, "I have prayed constantly for each one in our household while I nursed them. But God has not chosen to heed my pleadings."

Ruth looked stricken, and I hurried on, "But He did answer me once before when I prayed for my sons' health, and who knows, perhaps He will again. I will certainly be praying for him."

Mahlon lay quietly sleeping. His face was warm with the illness, but not as hot as the others had been as they had fought all restraint and tossed deliriously in their torment, and not as hot as he would become as the night deepened, unless the Lord did heed my cry and deliver him. Now, because there was nothing we could do immediately for Mahlon, I took the time to tell Ruth the story of my sons' early illnesses, and of the trip to Shiloh, and of Chilion's amazing healing.

"But if He can stop illness, why does He not do it now?

Why does He let this happen? You belong to Him, and you have lost your husband and one son. Surely He could spare your only remaining son!"

Mahlon's eyes opened then, and he looked at us, but without comprehension. And then we had no more time to discuss the ways of the Lord in dealing with illness as we fought against the illness ourselves.

It was some time later when I remembered Orpah. Surely she was all right, but I remembered the horror mirrored in her eyes as she fled, and I summoned Achsah, the overworked servant girl. "Tell me, Achsah, where is Orpah? Does she seem well?"

"Oh, Mistress, I did not know what to do! Orpah went out just before darkness fell, and she has not come back. I wanted to tell you, but you were so busy, and you have so much to bear. Surely, all is well with her?" But her voice held the fearful question that my own heart asked. Where is she? Why did she not return to the house?

"We will have to make sure." I tried to keep my voice even and calm, but I was again filled with anger. Could not Orpah behave reasonably and so have spared us this? "Tell Hazor that he is to go to the house of her brother and check. Perhaps Orpah wanted to be with her mother and brother tonight. We will do nothing further until he has returned."

I really doubted that Orpah was with her family. She had been so distraught and could have gone almost anywhere. My mind raced in circles while my hands wrung out cold cloths to cool Mahlon's fevered face. He did not seem quite so hot as he had been a little earlier, and I allowed myself to hope that he might survive.

When Hazor returned a short time later, his face told the story. "Orpah's brother has not seen her. He sends his sympathy that Chilion has died and asks us to let him know when we find Orpah."

"But he does not offer to help," I commented caustically.

"No, Mistress."

"The search must begin at once. She must be outside the village. Rouse the other servants and hunt throughout the nearby hills. Hazor, I am putting you in charge."

As I turned back and met Ruth's questioning gaze, I added, "I just cannot go myself. I am needed here."

"No, of course not, Mother. They will surely find her nearby."

But my mind was far from easy about Orpah as I resumed my vigil over Mahlon.

It was some time later that the servants returned, unsuccessful. I had been wrestling with my conscience and the possibility that Orpah had gone to my own favorite spot of seclusion. After questioning the searchers, I was sure that they had not ventured that far, but as I tried to tell them the particular place where I wanted them to look, I could see that they did know the spot.

I gazed long at Mahlon, and then made my decision. He was restless, but unconscious, and he seemed to be holding his own. I would have to go myself and chance missing any return to consciousness or . . . , but I would not let my mind consider the possibility that I might return to find all life gone from his body.

With the decision made, I was eager, even desperate to be off so that I could return more quickly. Hazor accompanied me. He carried a torch, but most of our way the moon provided all the light that we needed.

When we finally reached the clearing, a quick glance showed no sign of Orpah, and my heart sank. I had been so sure that I would find her here. Hazor lifted the torch high, and I caught just a glimpse of something white. Quickly, I pointed, and he brought the torch closer.

And there, wrapped in her robe, lay Orpah in the shadow of a large rock. My heart leapt in relief, but I knelt quietly and spoke gently to her lest I should startle her. Her face was waxen in the flickering light of the torch, and my heart stirred with pity.

I had spoken a second time and gently touched her shoulder before she roused and then awoke with a start.

"Orpah, it is I, your mother Naomi. Do not be afraid."

She looked about her, clearly puzzled at her surroundings. Then she began to remember, and her face crumpled. "Mahlon, is he also . . . ?"

"He was still alive when I left, but we must hurry. I need to get back and help Ruth to care for him."

But Orpah could not hurry. She had been overworked the last several days, as had we all, but now that the crisis was over for her, and her dear husband was dead, the strength built on anxiety was gone. She was utterly spent, and her steps lagged.

Finally, I could bear that snail's pace no longer. "Hazor, you see Orpah safely home. I will go ahead. The moon is bright, and I know the way." And I darted off, giving neither of them a chance to argue.

I arrived home panting and raced into the room where Mahlon lay, utterly disheveled and anxious. Ruth looked up from Mahlon, and the fear in her eyes sent a shock of horror through my soul. Was I too late?

But her words showed my fears to be amiss, as were hers. "Orpah," she gasped. "What happened?"

"Oh, she is well. But she could not hurry, so Hazor is bringing her. She was there in the clearing fast asleep." There was some bitterness in my voice as I asked, "Am I too late?"

But Ruth hurried to reassure me in turn. "Mahlon has been conscious briefly. He asked for you and was very upset that he could not speak to you. But see, he is awakening now!"

As Mahlon's eyes focused on Ruth and then on me, I was sure that I saw recognition and understanding there. And then he spoke, but his words were so faint that we had to bend close to hear.

"Mother, should I survive, we will go back to Bethlehem immediately. I was wrong in not going before. But if I die, what will become of you? If you were in Bethlehem, some of our relatives could care for you."

"We will be well, my son. The Lord God will provide for us. And we will return to Bethlehem. Do not fear for us." I clasped his hand so tightly that he winced in pain.

Then he spoke again, and I could tell that it was a real effort for him to form the words. "Mother," his voice was scarcely a whisper, "we never did take part in the worship of Chemosh. I did many things of which I am ashamed, but that we did not do."

His words brought such a flood of relief that I could not control the tears or steady my voice for speech, but I held his hand close against my cheek. Ruth sat crying, but silently, and she clasped his other hand. "Mother, Ruth, . . ." but his voice trailed off, and we never knew what he would have told us. For after his body had struggled valiantly against the sickness through half of the day and most of the night, he lost the battle.

I do not remember much of the following days. I took to my bed. The bodies of my sons were not given the proper Jewish burial. There were too many bodies to be taken care of. Many even shared a common grave.

Mahlon's death ended the sickness in our household, and only a few more people died in the village. The plague was over, and with it my hopes and dreams.

I had lost not only my sons but also all hope of children to carry on the name of my husband. I had not only no one to care for me but also no one who needed me to care for them.

Why could I not have died of the plague? Why should I be left on earth with nothing for which to live?

I lay on my mat in a quiet room and prayed to die. But, instead, I slept. For five days I slept, only to awaken and eat or drink something of what was brought to me, and then to sleep again.

I do not know how long I would have continued thus if I had not overheard Ruth and Orpah in conversation in the courtyard. Orpah was saying, "But she has to know!" And her voice was raised in argument. That was so unusual that my attention was caught.

Ruth's reply was softer, but now I was listening closely. "Yes, I know, but I cannot bring myself to tell her."

Then perhaps realizing how close to my window they were they moved away, and I could not hear. But I had to know. Clearly, it was bad news, but I could not lie there idle and let them face it alone.

I arose and washed with the water left close by my mat. As I pulled on my clothing, I trembled all over from weakness. I sat on my low stool until I felt somewhat steadied, and then I left the room and joined my daughters-in-law in the courtyard.

Ruth's and Orpah's loving greetings were all that any mother could ask, and I felt a oneness among us that we had not shared before.

Finally I turned to Ruth. "I overheard part of your conversation this morning. Tell me, my dear, what has gone wrong now?"

She hesitated, but I insisted, "I am strong enough to bear it, whatever it is. Anyway, it cannot compare to the trouble that we have already faced."

"No, of course not, but it is trouble. Jarmuth, the under shepherd, was alone caring for the sheep when Mahlon came in ill." She took a deep breath and fought for control of her voice before she continued, "His body was found yesterday. They think that he also died of the plague. He had been dead for some time, and the animals had torn at his body. The sheep are scattered, and we do not know how many are even alive.

I drew in my breath. This was indeed trouble. The loss of the sheep was a calamity. They would have paid our way back to Bethlehem and provided for our needs when we arrived. Unless they could be regathered, we were destitute.

"Call Hazor," I directed. "He will tell us who can help us find the sheep."

Hazor came, but his words were not encouraging. "I will try to find someone to help, but I do not think many will be willing. So many people have died, and some are saying that your family bears the responsibility for bringing the plague upon us. They say that your God is punishing you. They do not feel friendly toward you. But I will try."

Hazor's warning proved to have been justified. No one was willing to help us hunt our sheep. But by the time he had returned, I had another plan. I allowed him to give his gloomy report and then set my next plan in motion.

"Hazor, would you be willing to help gather the sheep?" His affirmation was unhesitating, and I knew that he was not one of those who felt unfriendly toward us.

"Orpah, Ruth, would you like to help, or would you rather keep things going here?"

After a brief consultation, it was agreed that Orpah would run the house while Ruth would join Hazor and me in the hills.

Gone was my lethargy. There was too much that needed doing for me to spend any more time in bed. And while the deep grief remained, the hopelessness had fled.

*   *   *

"How I praise You, my Lord, that You knew I needed work to bring me out of my self-pity. I thank You that You can use bad things to accomplish good."

Naomi smiled as she remembered those days of work out in the hills of Moab, work that she had enjoyed and that had brought a measure of peace to her soul.

And eventually she again slept, dreaming of the hills near Bethlehem and of the days of her girlhood when she had watched the sheep grazing there.

10

▼▲▼▲▼▲▼▲

*T*HE RIVER CROSSING WAS ACCOMPLISHED, at least
for Naomi and Ruth. It had been a raucous, noisy
scene. The men had girded up their robes, tucking
the back of the robe firmly into the belt in front, making
what was essentially breeches of the long flowing robes.
Thus garbed, they could wade into the Jordan unhindered
by heavy wet garments.

Naomi and Ruth had been among the first brought
across. They stood on the west bank, watching the men
bringing across the last of the beasts. Ruth eagerly took in
all the excitement, but Naomi's mind was in a fever of impatience to be on their way west, down the road to Bethlehem.

Now, partly because the caravan was nearing journey's
end, and partly because the men enjoyed a break from routine, the fording was accomplished in a spirit of boisterous
gaiety. To Naomi they seemed to be playing more than
working. Certainly, they were not hurrying. Ruth's joyous
laugh burst out as the men frolicked and splashed in the
water, and Naomi forced a smile. She, herself, had been
overjoyed this morning when her feet had touched the soil

of Israel for the first time in 10 years. She had fallen to her knees and kissed the earth while tears of joy rained down. Now she tried to regain that joy and to relax. She knew she could not hurry them any with her impatience, but it seemed a long wait until all were assembled and prepared to travel. At last Shedeur's voice rang out with the call to move ahead.

As they began to walk, Naomi felt the tension ease. I have been hurrying for so long that I do not know how to be at ease, she realized. Those busy days of regathering the sheep and preparation for the trip left no time for relaxing.

The gathering of the sheep had been difficult. Not only were the sheep widely scattered, but also the winter winds and rain had kept the searchers soaked and cold much of the time. And yet, as Naomi looked back, she realized that she had found comfort in those dreary days.

I was doing something—something important, and I was outside again, working with sheep as I had as a child. At first my muscles cried out in torment against the unaccustomed exercise, but then they strengthened, and it was pure joy to feel strong and fit and able to do what needed doing.

We formed a team, Ruth, Hazor, and myself. I found both of those Moabites to be kind and helpful. For Ruth, as well as for myself, it was a healing experience. There was little time for self-pity as we hunted the sheep.

But in another way our search was very disappointing. Of the original large flock, we saved only 50 sheep. Several of the sheep had obviously become meals for the bears and lions that always roamed the hills.

But most of them disappeared without a trace. We were sure that they had been stolen, and we also knew whose flock was greatly increased. But we had no way to prove our suspicions. Had Mahlon or Chilion been alive, it would have been a simple matter. Either of them could have called to our sheep, and they would have quickly separated from the other flock and returned to their own shepherd. But their shepherds were dead, and they did not know our voices.

· We spent six days in the hills, searching and re-gathering those few scraggly sheep. We knew that we must sell what we had quickly as we could not watch the sheep adequately and also do the work at the house. Several shepherds were willing to buy our tiny flock, and in the end, Ruth's father purchased them for a fair price.

Now the die was cast. We must quickly make our plans to return to Bethlehem.

Rejoining Orpah in the house, we set to work, sorting out what things we could take, what we could sell, and what must be discarded. When the accumulation of items that we wanted to take grew too large, we had to re-sort and leave all but the necessities. With our limited means, I knew that I should only plan for one pack animal, but after setting aside all that we could, I knew that I would have to secure a second beast.

As we worked together packing and sorting, we also shed tears together. Our losses were fresh in our minds, and each item seemed to carry some memory wrapped inside it. I tried to comfort my daughters-in-law that an all-wise God was in control, and that He would provide for us.

One day Ruth burst out, almost angrily, "How can you bear it? You have lost your husband and both your sons? Why do you still trust your God to provide and care for you?"

Orpah had also lifted her head and was waiting for my answer. I hesitated, knowing that a good deal might rest on my answer. "Ruth, I do not know how to explain my faith in the Almighty God. I cannot tell you why He does the things He does, and why He allowed me to lose my husband and my sons. But I do know that He 'keeps His covenant and His lovingkindness to a thousandth generation with those who love Him and keep His commandments.'

"The Law says, 'Then it shall come about, because you listen to these judgments and keep and do them, that the Lord your God will keep with you His covenant and His lovingkindness which He swore to your forefathers. And He will love you and bless you and multiply you.'

"God has always kept His promises to His people, and I believe He will do so now."

Some days later word came from Kir-haraseth that a caravan from Israel had passed through. The word was that the drought was over in my homeland. The early rains had come on schedule, and it had continued to rain throughout the winter. It seemed likely that the latter rains would also fall and insure a bountiful harvest. Even now Israel was lush and green, according to the report.

To me the message was bittersweet; it was too late for Elimelech, Mahlon, and Chilion. But now we could go back, knowing that food would soon be plentiful. I could imagine the joy that my friends in Bethlehem were feeling, and I was even more eager to be among them.

The caravan that had journeyed south through Kir-haraseth would go on to Ezion-geber on the Red Sea and then begin the return journey, again passing through Kir-haraseth in about a month's time. I was determined to travel back to Bethlehem with this caravan.

With new impetus, we worked, and as we did our daily tasks, I told my daughters-in-law of my homeland. Ruth made a real effort to listen and respond. But Orpah showed little interest in anything. I knew that both girls were grieving, of course, and I understood their grief. My own heart was broken, but I knew I must plan for the future. Only in that way could I bear the changes in my life. So I tried to interest them in future plans, also, that their healing might be hastened. I think that Ruth understood this and tried to find the same hope for herself.

But poor Orpah! She seemed to be a crumpled flower that could not regain her vitality. During those days when

Ruth and I had been out in the hills, Orpah had been alone. While she had plenty to do, her work had not kept her mind completely occupied as ours had. Talk of Israel now, rather than encouraging her, seemed to fill her soul with a new dread.

Surely time will bring her healing, I assured myself. But I worried and did not know how to help her.

What items from the house that we could, we sold, adding the coins to our meager supply of silver. The house itself could not be sold. It would stand empty until someone decided to move in, and then it would belong to them.

Then the day came to leave for Kir-haraseth. The caravan might not be back for a week, but we must not miss it. Now was the time to go. We loaded our pack animals with some difficulty, but the unwieldy packs stayed in place when the patient beasts moved. We would be in Kir-haraseth before nightfall and would stay there at an inn until the caravan came through.

Ruth and I kept up a steady conversation as we walked, while Orpah trudged along between us in silence. Only when asked a direct question did she answer.

I watched her, and the question that I had kept pushing away would no longer be denied. Was I doing right in taking these young girls away from their homeland and their families, to a new country, a country where they would be treated as strangers? I knew that they would face trials in Israel. My people had no high opinion of Moabites.

They were both young and comely. If they stayed in Moab, they would remarry, raise families, and have normal lives. But if they continued with me, they might regret it for the rest of their lives.

They were loyal, and they had assumed that their place as my daughters-in-law was to go with me. But I must not be selfish and keep them. But how could I let them go? They were all the family that I had left! And if they remained here, they would never learn to worship the true God.

Silently I struggled against the decision that I knew I must make. Ruth glanced at me several times, uneasy at my sudden silence. But Orpah was too preoccupied to even notice.

I realized that I could prolong this no longer. I could not take two daughters to Israel who would be happier in Moab. Abruptly, I stopped, breathing a prayer for strength. "Ruth, Orpah, go back; you must each return to your mother's house. And may the Lord deal kindly with you as you have dealt with my dead sons and with me. May the Lord grant that you may find rest, each of you in the house of your husband."

Quickly, I embraced and kissed each of them, giving them no opportunity to answer. And as I held them, I wept. Their tears mingled with mine, and I was somewhat comforted that the parting would be difficult for them also.

But then Ruth said, "No, we will surely return with you to your people," and Orpah nodded in agreement.

My heart felt near to breaking, but I could not let them make this sacrifice for me. "No, return, my daughters. Why should you go with me? Have I yet sons in my womb, that they may be your husbands? Return, my daughters! Go back, for I am too old to have a husband. But even if I did have hope—if I had a husband right now and were to bear sons, would you wait until they were grown? Would you refrain from marrying all that time? No, my daughters; this is harder for me than it is for you. The hand of the Lord has gone forth against me in bringing me all this sorrow, but you must not stay with me."

My insistence caused them to cry harder than ever, but Orpah obediently kissed me good-bye and turned back down the road toward her home.

Then I turned to Ruth to bid her good-bye, also, but she threw her arms around me and held on tight.

"Ruth, my dear, look, your sister-in-law has gone back to her people and her gods; you must go back with her."

But Ruth continued to cling to me, and her words were soothing to my troubled heart. "Do not urge me to leave you or to turn back from following you, my mother; for where you go, I will go, and where you live, I will live. Your people shall be my people, and your God, my God. Where you die, I will die, and there I will be buried. May God punish me severely if anything but death parts you and me."

My heart beat with joy so that I could not speak, but I turned, and, with her hand in mine, we started on down the road.

All the rest of the journey to Kir-haraseth, my heart sang with the words, "Your people shall be my people and your God, my God. . . ."

When we arrived at the inn in Kir-haraseth, it was to discover that the caravan would arrive the next day. There was no time for relaxing that night; I feverishly planned and figured. Would the silver be enough to see us settled in Bethlehem? Would the caravan be willing to take us along? Would I be able to keep up with the caravan? What supplies should I buy? Through the night the questions raced through my mind, and I was thankful to see the morning light.

Quickly Ruth and I bought what added provisions we had decided that we would need for the journey. Then during the afternoon the city buzzed with the information that the caravan had arrived.

As quickly as possible, I made my way to Shedeur, the caravan's leader. His expression was forbidding and his eyes grim. My hands trembled as I asked that we be allowed to accompany his caravan to Bethlehem.

"Women are a terrible nuisance on a trip," he began, "always whining and lagging behind. They get sick; they cannot pitch a tent; they are afraid of their shadow!"

I could see that he was just getting warmed up to his subject, so I interrupted, quite rudely, I am afraid. But my courage was fleeing, and I must speak while I still could. "I expected to pay our way."

"What did you say?" He had been busy with his tirade, but his ears had caught the reference to money, I was sure.

"I said, 'I expected to pay our way.'"

He looked at me shrewdly. "I would have to charge a high price to take two women along." And he named a sum that took my breath away.

"But that is more than I have!" I protested with a sinking heart.

"Well, how much do you have?" he asked gruffly.

After I had told him, I wished that I had held my tongue, for he grumpily lowered his price to that exact figure.

"But how can I arrive in Bethlehem with nothing left?"

"That is your problem. I have set my price, and little enough it is, too, for taking two women alone, women without even a man to look after them!"

"So be it," I acquiesced, handing him the silver and watching him count it. "We must get back to Bethlehem. When do you leave?"

"At first light in the morning. And if you are late, you will be left." And he walked off.

As I hurried back to the inn and Ruth, I wondered if I had done the right thing. That rascal had tricked me into telling him just how much silver I had. I was sure that he would have settled for less if I had had less. But the important thing was to get back to Bethlehem. Surely the Lord would not allow us to starve after we got there. I could sell the donkeys when our journey was ended.

At the inn I told Ruth the news, and she sputtered with me over the greedy Shedeur. But she made a good suggestion, "Let us go out and join the caravan tonight, my mother. Then he cannot find an excuse to leave us behind."

And so it was that that evening we had joined the caravan. And the journey home was begun in the morning.

* * *

Now they were less than a day's journey from Bethlehem! Old Shedeur had proved to be a fair leader and did not allow any of the men in the caravan to bother Naomi or Ruth. Naomi thought perhaps the tough crust that he showed to the world was hiding a softer heart beneath. While she and Ruth could not do a man's work, they did gather firewood and kindling, carry water, and all the other chores they could handle.

And they had kept up. Those days up on the hills, searching for sheep, had helped to strengthen them both. The caravan had never been slowed because of them.

Now Naomi's step was sedate, but in her heart she was skipping like a little girl. She was near home! She was a poor widow; she did not know the future, but she was going home!

"Thank You, God of my fathers, that Ruth came with me, and especially that she has chosen You to be her God. And please, Lord God, watch over Orpah. Give her a husband who will care for her and a houseful of children for whom she can care. May she remember what she learned of You. And thank You for this journey, for the time I have had to reflect on Your goodness."

11

*I*T WAS THE LAST DAY of the trip. Naomi's eyes took in all the familiar surroundings. Each bush and tree seemed to shout, "Home!" Each rock was a part of her homeland.

She knew that her body was tired after the long days of walking and the short nights. In fact, last night she had slept very little.

And today she felt marvelous—young and strong. She knew it was the excitement and happiness.

It seems wrong, somehow, to be happy, Naomi reflected. I have lost my beloved husband, and I miss him terribly even now. I have lost my only sons, and that wound is still deep and painful, yet my heart can rejoice in being home.

I wonder what Ruth is feeling. She cannot know the joy that I feel in coming home. But perhaps she, too, knows the happiness of journey's end. And I know that she is full of hope. She is so much like me in that. Neither of us can bear the thought of a grim, bleak future, so in our minds we paint it bright and cheerful. And while we may be disappointed, at least we have had the joy of expecting the good.

"My mother," Ruth interrupted Naomi's reverie, "what are those flowers? Are they not lovely?"

"Yes, aren't they! Those are the lilies of the field. Every spring they burst into bloom for just a few days, and then they are gone. But while they last, they give so much beauty.

"Ruth, are you happy? Do you feel excited at your new adventure?"

Ruth paused in her walk. "Would you understand if I told you that in spite of my pain in losing Mahlon, I am experiencing a joy that I have never known before?"

She continued as they walked on, "I think that it is partly because I now belong to the Lord Jehovah. I do not know what lies ahead, but I am sure that the Lord will care for me. I am happy to be one of the people of the true God, and I am eager for you to teach me more of His ways."

Naomi hugged her impulsively. "Ruth, I am so glad! I asked because I myself am experiencing such joy. So I understand completely. I do not think that our love for Mahlon and the others is less because we can enjoy the goodness of God now. It would serve no purpose for us to live in the past.

"Have I ever told you about Job, my dear?"

"You have mentioned him, but I do not know his story, Mother."

So Naomi began the narrative. "Job was a righteous man who lived in the times of our fathers.

"He was a very rich man with many camels, sheep, oxen, and donkeys. He also had many servants and seven sons and three daughters.

"One day Satan declared to God that Job only served Him because God had blessed him with such abundance. So God allowed Satan to test Job by taking away his riches. In one day he lost all his camels, sheep, oxen, and donkeys, all his servants, and even his sons and daughters.

"Even while Job grieved, he worshiped God and said, 'Naked I came from my mother's womb, And naked I shall return there. The Lord gave and the Lord has taken away. Blessed be the name of the Lord.' He refused to be angry with God.

"Then God pointed out Job's righteous attitude to Satan, and Satan asked a further test. 'He is still healthy,' he said. 'Let me "touch his bone and his flesh; he will curse Thee to Thy face!"'

"So God let Satan afflict Job's body, and Job broke out in boils from the top of his head to the soles of his feet. His wife railed at him, and his friends accused him of being a great sinner that God should treat him thus."

"That poor man," Ruth sympathized. "At least we have good health."

"Yes, that is so. Well, Job began to question God and to ask why these things happened. He told God that he was too good to deserve all this. His moods fluctuated wildly, and he even declared that he wished he had never been born, yet he never gave up his trust in God. He told his friends, 'Though He slay me, I will hope in Him.'

"At the end of many days God spoke to Job. He asked him how he dared to argue against the One who made all things. At last Job saw things in perspective; he saw the greatness of God, and that showed him how small and unworthy he was. He cried out to God, 'I repent in dust and ashes.'

"And then after Job had learned and profited from his terrible time of suffering, God gave him comfort and wealth through his brothers and sisters. In the end he had twice as many camels, sheep, oxen, and donkeys. And the Lord gave him seven more sons and three more daughters and a long life besides."

Naomi, ending the story, was silent. Job was like a dear friend to her. His story had been her comfort since the death of Elimelech.

"Oh, what a wonderful story!" Ruth exclaimed. She hesitated and then asked softly, "Do you think that is why you have suffered, because God wanted to show that your faith is true?"

"Oh, my dear," Naomi's voice was sorrowful, "my faith was not strong like Job's. God would never have pointed me out as an example of righteousness. No, I am sure that I have brought much of my sadness upon myself. I was self-willed and not willing to trust God to provide for my family during the famine. I persuaded my husband to go to Moab against his better judgment. The only way that I am like Job is that I have learned to know my God better through my suffering—and I have repented of my lack of faith."

Ruth clasped her mother-in-law's hand and added, "And perhaps we will be like Job in being richly blessed after the time of suffering is over. Do you suppose?"

Naomi smiled at her hopeful spirit, and they walked on in companionable silence. Around them were the fields. Some were wheat, and they were lush and green, with the heads not yet ripened. But the barley fields were white, their heads of grain ripe and full. In a few of the barley fields the reapers were already laboring. Before many more days all of the barley fields would be full of reapers.

The sun was around to the west, but still high in the sky, when they topped the little hill that gave them their first view of Bethlehem. How beautiful it looked, nestled among the green hills and the green and white pattern of the grain fields! For a moment Naomi stopped to let her eyes feast on the well-loved village. Ruth, also, took in the panorama.

"That is Bethlehem, Ruth," Naomi spoke softly, almost reverently, "Bethlehem, the 'place of blessing'! Home!" and her tone became one of exultation.

Eagerly, she clasped Ruth's hand and started down the little hill, almost running. Her steps continued the brisk pace for a time, and then, almost imperceptibly, they slowed.

What will people think? Will they scorn me because we went to Moab? We were among the wealthy, and now I return in poverty. We had the blessing of God upon our family, and now I have nothing and no one. What will they say? Even my name is a mockery now. Pleasant! There is nothing pleasant about my life! I should rather be called Mara, because, like the waters of that pool called Marah, my life has been bitter and caused pain to those who needed me.

Her thoughts took another turn. Is Cousin Leah still alive? Oh, how I pray that she is! But will she forgive me? Has time softened her heart? Or will she accuse me of causing Elimelech's death? And Mahlon's and Chilion's. She never did like me; will she hate me now?

Where will we live? How will we buy food? she thought. And as the burden of the future rested heavily upon her shoulders, she lost the joy of returning to the "place of blessing." I wonder if my time of suffering is nearly over, or perhaps is it just beginning?

"O Lord," Naomi's lips moved, but the words were silent, "I am afraid. I do not know what will happen now. And I am not nearly as strong as I would like to think. But, Lord, You are strong. Whatever happens, I trust You."

She took a deep breath and straightened her shoulders. They were entering Bethlehem, and she would not wear her fear like a cloak for all the world to see. If her hands were clenched and her heart aflutter, no one would know but the Lord, and He would understand. Resolutely, she lifted her head and smiled encouragingly at Ruth.

The caravan would stop at the village well. As it was the cool of the day, the women would soon be coming to draw water. Surely she would see someone she knew, and she could make inquiries.

But Naomi had forgotten how quickly news travels along the caravan trail. Yesterday word had come to Bethlehem that the caravan was near, and that Naomi was with it.

And that accompanying her was a strange girl. The women of Bethlehem had busily discussed this information, remembering and reminding one another of events in Naomi's past. And they had speculated on her circumstances now.

So when Naomi and Ruth walked up to the well area, it was to find a crowd gathered there. Then an almost familiar voice cried out, "Naomi, is it really you?" There were hurried footsteps, and strong arms wrapped around her. She was kissed fervently on either cheek, and then the woman stepped back to look at her more closely.

And now Naomi could in turn study her. "Deborah?" she asked hesitantly. "Oh, Deborah, it is so good to see you!"

Then the other women crowded around. "Is this really Naomi?"

"But where is Elimelech? Where are her sons?"

"Naomi, we thought never to see you again. It has been so long!"

"Naomi, you have changed so much. I would never have known you!"

At last Naomi could bear it no longer, and she burst out, "Do not call me Naomi; call me Mara, for the Almighty has dealt very bitterly with me. I went out full, but the Lord has brought me back empty. Why do you call me Naomi, since the Lord has witnessed against me and the Almighty has afflicted me?"

Her words silenced the strident voices, and all drew back except Deborah. Her arm slipped around Naomi's waist and she said, "Come, sit here on the bench, and I will draw you a drink." Then as she looked toward the well and the buzz of activity there, she added, "No, I will give you a drink from what I drew earlier. I am so glad that I drew my water while we waited. It will be late before the men are finished watering the camels and donkeys."

Moving quickly as she spoke, she handed Naomi a dripping cup of water, still cold from the well. Naomi drank it thirstily. She had forgotten how good the water from home was.

Then she stopped abruptly. Still holding the cup, she said, "Deborah, this is my daughter-in-law Ruth. She was Mahlon's wife, and she is very dear to me." She smiled at Ruth and added, "Deborah and I were best friends when we were girls."

Deborah's words to Ruth were kind although her manner was hesitant. But she quickly gave the younger woman a drink from her jar also. Then she said to Naomi, "You must stay with Caleb and me tonight. That will give you time to make plans. Caleb will know what is best for you to do."

"That would be wonderful—but wait! I must know! Is Cousin Leah yet alive?" Naomi waited with bated breath for Deborah's answer.

Deborah looked puzzled. "Yes, she lives." Then as Naomi breathed a sigh of relief, she went on, "But I do not remember your ever being so anxious about old Leah. I did not think that you got along well with her."

"I did not, but I must see her now. I have much to say to her, and I was so afraid that she would not be alive when I returned."

"Indeed, she is not well. Naomi, you would not be harsh with a sick old woman?"

"Oh, no, I do not want to rebuke her. Rather I would beg her pardon for the wrongs that I have done her. Does she still live in her own house?"

Deborah looked even more perplexed, but she replied, "Yes, come, and I will take you to her now. Are these your beasts of burden?" She quickly loosed the two donkeys, and the three women started down the street that seemed both familiar, and yet changed, to Naomi.

The two older women chatted eagerly, catching up on the news of Bethlehem. Tactfully, Deborah waited for Naomi to volunteer her own story when she was ready.

Naomi grew quiet as they neared Cousin Leah's house. Even from a distance it looked to be in poor repair. What had happened? Was not Cousin Reuben looking after things?

Then they were at the door, and Deborah said, "Ruth and I will wait for you outside while you speak with her, Naomi."

Naomi's courage nearly failed her, but she knew this would grow no easier with waiting. Without a word she knocked on the side post of the open door and then entered.

"Who is there?" asked a querulous old voice.

"It is I, Naomi, Cousin Leah. Peace be on you."

Cousin Leah, now becoming visible to Naomi as her eyes adjusted to the dimness of the house, reclined on a mat in the corner of the room. She tried to raise herself to get a better look at her visitor, sure that she could not have heard correctly. Naomi crossed to her quickly and knelt beside her. She clasped her hand and bent to kiss the wrinkled cheeks.

"Who did you say you were?" asked the old woman again.

"I am Naomi, wife of Elimelech." She waited to see if Cousin Leah would comprehend.

But Leah's sharp mind had not forsaken her. She was only shocked to see Naomi so unexpectedly. She was so shaken, in fact, that she completely forgot to return the normal greeting, but demanded instead, "And where is Elimelech? Has he no time for an old woman?"

"Elimelech is dead, as are Mahlon and Chilion. And I am come back alone except for my daughter-in-law Ruth." Naomi had decided that she might as well tell all the bad news at once.

"Dead?" Leah's voice trembled as she repeated the word. "All of them?"

Naomi nodded. There was silence as the old woman struggled to assimilate this information.

Finally, Naomi spoke again. "I came to you as soon as I got back to ask your pardon for my unkindness to you in the past. The Lord has dealt very harshly with me, and He has made me realize how I sinned against you. Will you forgive me?"

Cousin Leah was astounded. Where was the proud, haughty Naomi that she had known? But when she spoke her voice was harsh. "You were a cruel young thing! You thought yourself too good to accept help from me. You were so selfish that you could not bear to share your family or your happiness with your husband's kinswoman. Now the Lord has brought you down, and you want help from the one you formerly despised."

Naomi tried to interrupt, that this was not why she had come, but the older woman was not to be stopped. "You can stay here," she continued as if Naomi had not spoken, "but I will withhold judgment on what kind of woman you have become until I have watched you awhile."

At last Naomi could speak. "I did not come here to ask your help, Cousin Leah," she said firmly. "I only came for your forgiveness. I want there to be peace between us."

Her voice had trembled while she spoke, but she stiffened as Leah answered, "So you are still too proud to let me help!" She laughed. "I thought that you had not really changed so much."

Naomi was taken aback. She sat in silence, considering the other woman's words. Cousin Leah seemed determined to misunderstand her, but how could she prove the other woman wrong except by staying here? And Cousin Leah really did need her help! Certainly, there appeared to be plenty that could be done.

After a few moments she spoke, "Cousin Leah, I would be honored to live in your house. But you remember that I have Ruth with me. Where I stay, she stays. Do you want us both?"

"Want has nothing to do with it," she snapped. "You are Elimelech's widow, and you belong with me. That girl will have to stay here too," she added grudgingly. Then she looked at Naomi suspiciously, "What kind of a girl is she?"

"Ruth is a lovely girl from Moab."

"A heathen!" she exclaimed. "You brought a heathen girl back to Israel?" In her excitement she tried again to sit up, and then she collapsed back onto her mat, breathing hard.

"Cousin Leah, please listen. Ruth is a Moabite, but she has chosen our people over her own, and she worships the Lord Jehovah rather than the gods of her people."

"I do not know what people will say of me, keeping a heathen foreigner here!" Her voice quavered resignedly, "But I know my duty. You will both live here with me. Who cares if I lose my friends?" On this note of self-pity she subsided and closed her eyes as if to sleep.

Naomi sat by her a few minutes more, her emotions churning. It certainly would not be easy to live here, but it seemed to be God's provision of a house. They would still need food; she was sure just by looking about her that Cousin Leah had no extra to provide for two more people. Well, that could wait until tomorrow. Now she must go tell Ruth and Deborah of this change of plan.

She emerged into the sunshine with some relief and found Deborah and Ruth engaged in lively conversation. All the stiffness was gone from Deborah's manner, and Ruth, also, seemed at ease. As she watched them together, a sudden thought struck her. I did not tell Cousin Leah that I have returned impoverished. What if she is expecting me to provide for her also? Well, that, too, will have to wait. We can stay tonight at least. But tomorrow I will be sure that she understands our condition.

She came out of her reverie to find Deborah and Ruth both looking at her in concern. Before either could ask a question, Naomi spoke. "Cousin Leah has asked us to stay here with her—at least for tonight. It will not be easy, Ruth, but I feel that we must.

"Deborah, I thank you for your offer of hospitality. It is so good to have you as my friend!" Tears were very close today, and Naomi struggled to retain her composure as she and her old friend embraced.

"I will not trouble you today with questions," Deborah murmured, "but when you are ready, I want to hear your story."

Naomi clasped her hand convulsively and gave her a teary smile. Then together she and Ruth watched Deborah walk briskly toward her own house. They turned to the pressing duties of the evening.

The packs were first unloaded from the donkeys, which were then tethered in a patch of lush grass. There was not enough water in the house for the thirsty beasts, and from the leanness of their flanks, Naomi was sure that no one had watered them while the caravan was at the well.

"I will go get more water, Mother," Ruth offered. "I remember the way we came." And she hurried off with the jars.

Naomi set to work preparing the evening meal. She and Ruth had some raisin cakes left from their travel provisions and some parched grain also. She checked Cousin Leah's stores and found some meal and a little oil. Quickly, she put sticks inside the earthen jar that was used for baking and then moved a blazing ember from the open fire into the jar. Soon the jar would be hot enough to bake their flat bread. As it heated she stirred up the ingredients and shaped the dough into several small flat cakes. It would be good to have a home-cooked meal even though it was humble.

Before she had finished, Ruth returned and watered the donkeys. As the bread baked on the outside of the hot jar, Naomi roused Cousin Leah and carefully washed her hands. Then she helped her to eat before she and Ruth ate their meal together in the courtyard.

When they were finished, she entered the little house and lit the lamp. Then she led Ruth over to Cousin Leah and presented her to the testy old lady. Cousin Leah looked the girl over and then said, "Peace be on you. I hope you will be happy here. But how you can be without a man to care for you and protect you, I do not know." Then as if regretting this brief lapse into kindness, she turned her face to the wall and ignored Ruth's returning of the customary greeting.

Quietly, Ruth and Naomi cleared up their dishes and rolled out their mats for rest. It was their first night under a roof in nearly a week. But as Naomi looked up, she smiled. She was under a roof, but still a star twinkled at her. That hole will have to be repaired before the early rains, she thought.

"O Lord, there is so much to do, and things are still so uncertain. But we are home, and we have a house to live in. And people have been unexpectedly kind. I thank You for all of these things, and thank You for Deborah, my friend. . . ."

And Naomi was asleep.

12

NAOMI AWOKE AT FIRST LIGHT, feeling refreshed and alert. As she rejoiced in the well-being that was flooding her mind and body, it dawned on her that she had slept the night through.

"Thank You, Lord," she whispered, "and thank You for this new day." She stretched luxuriously and sat up. Quietly, she left her mat, and stepping carefully to avoid Ruth's still sleeping figure, she removed the bar and opened the door of the house. The sun had not yet risen, but the growing light crept in to make the dim room a little brighter.

Naomi stepped outside to enjoy the freshness of the morning and then walked around the house to open the shutters of the single window. Today will be a busy day, Naomi thought. I must talk to Cousin Leah about my own poverty. We must make some plans for our support, and I absolutely must give this house a thorough cleaning.

I do wonder what happened to Reuben? He was supposed to be caring for Cousin Leah. But 10 years is a long time. I am sure neither he nor Elimelech dreamed that his job would endure so long.

And someone has been providing for Cousin Leah, at least partially. There was a little food in the house last night, and it is obvious that Cousin Leah had not been looking after her own needs. She seems to be completely bedfast.

As these thoughts passed through her mind, the enormity of the task that she had taken on and the uncertainties of her life assailed Naomi. "O Lord God, how will I ever manage? Ruth is a stranger here and little more than a child, and Cousin Leah is completely helpless—all but that still sharp tongue. I do not see how I can ever do all that is needed. And how can I be patient and kind when she cuts me down at every opportunity? I am trusting You, my God, to show me the way and to lead me in it."

Just then one of the donkeys brayed his greeting to the day. His companion joined him, and for a few moments the air rang with their discordant song.

"Aha, my fine friends," Naomi spoke aloud, "today, by the will of God, you will have new masters, and tomorrow you will announce the morning in someone else's yard." They had stood the trip well and were in good flesh. Perhaps one of them could be traded for a goat. She could then make cheese, and they would have plenty of milk. Perhaps more nourishing food would help Cousin Leah regain her strength.

Naomi added "sell the donkeys" to her mental list of things to be done today.

As she turned back toward the house, she saw Ruth standing in the doorway. They greeted one another, and Naomi thought, What a comely girl she is! I hope that my people will treat her with kindness!

They stepped back inside to get the food for their breakfast. They would have cold bread left from last night's baking and more of the raisins. Naomi was hungry for fresh fruit, but it would be three more months before she could enjoy that treat.

Cousin Leah slept on, so Naomi left her share of the meal inside while she and Ruth went back out to eat theirs in the courtyard.

"How I love the warm weather when we can be outside! I have never accustomed myself to eating and working inside where it is so dim and often smoky!" Naomi expressed her thoughts aloud.

"Yes," agreed Ruth. "This is much more pleasant. And it looks like another beautiful day. What are your plans for today?"

Naomi outlined the things that they must do, and they discussed the details together.

"As soon as Cousin Leah awakes, I would like you to help me move her outside. Then I can thoroughly clean the house while she gets some fresh air and sunshine.

"I want to wash all the clothing, blankets, and mats in the house too. I will take them down to the watering troughs by the well later on. That will have to wait until the house has been cleaned.

"Perhaps, we should go get water right away. If we both go, we can get enough to wash all the vessels and jars, both Cousin Leah's and our own. Ours are sure to be dusty from the trip."

So chatting cheerfully, the two woman journeyed to the well. Naomi was greeted by several other women who were also getting an early start on their day.

Some of the women Naomi recognized, and others looked familiar, but she could not recall their names. Everyone, of course, knew Naomi. The story of her arrival in Bethlehem with a Moabite daughter-in-law was important news.

As they walked back home, Naomi suggested, "Ruth, would you be willing to take the donkeys to market while I clean? If you can trade one for a milking goat, it would be well. And you could take either silver or food for the second one."

Ruth answered unhesitatingly, "Yes, I will be glad to take them. I will do my best bargaining."

Both women smiled at that. Despite Ruth's gentle manners and quiet ways, she was a shrewd bargainer and was seldom bested in a trade. "Ah, Ruth, I know that the matter is in good hands. If I could only handle Cousin Leah as successfully!"

When they set their jars down and entered the house, they found Cousin Leah awake and fretful. "Where have you been?" she snapped. "I thought I had been deserted again. I am hungry!" she added peevishly.

"We were getting water, Cousin Leah. Did you sleep well? We tried not to awaken you when we arose."

"I never sleep well! Now what are you doing?" as Naomi and Ruth made preparations for moving her outside.

"We are going to carry you outside into the courtyard so that you can enjoy the sunshine," Naomi replied gently. As she spoke, Naomi and Ruth carefully eased Cousin Leah onto a mat with poles slipped through each side. Then one at each end, they lifted the stretcher carefully, gently eased it through the doorway, and deposited the old lady in the shade of a sycamore tree.

Then Naomi sat beside her charge, murmuring to Ruth, "Would you bring her breakfast out, my dear?"

Leah had borne the move in silence and now lay blinking. As her eyes adjusted to the brightness of the day, she began looking around her. "This courtyard is a mess! And there is no garden planted! But if there were, those donkeys would have eaten it last night! When are you going to get rid of those noisy beasts?"

She stopped fussing to eat the food that Ruth had brought her, and Naomi was able to answer. "Ruth is going to take the donkeys to the market right now. And we will get the courtyard cleaned up. I think that lentils and beans will produce if I plant them right away. "Ruth," she called to the girl who was now untethering the donkeys, "see if you can get some beans and lentils for us to plant. Perhaps you could even find cucumber seeds or gourds."

Ruth agreed and set off with the animals.

Naomi turned back to her old cranky relative. "There are some other things that we need to discuss, Cousin Leah, before I set to work." She paused before continuing, "Did you realize that I have come home in poverty? I will do my best to provide food for all of us, but I want you to know that Elimelech's flocks are gone."

"I am not surprised," Cousin Leah replied. "No good ever comes of traipsing off to foreign countries. You remember that I warned you! What happened that you lost everything?"

So Naomi took the time to tell Elimelech's old cousin the story. And Naomi was amazed that the sad tale of the last 10 years could be told in such a few sentences.

Cousin Leah closed her eyes during the recital, and with those snapping black eyes closed, she looked a sad and tired old woman.

As Naomi ended, Cousin Leah did not open her eyes or make any response, so after a bit Naomi concluded that she wished to be left alone and rose silently to begin her work.

She took the broom from the corner and began her assault against the accumulated dirt. The broom was in poor condition, and she wished she had told Ruth to get a new one at the market. But perhaps she would best stick with this one until she knew if they could manage enough for the food they needed from the trading. First the walls were swept down, and then the hard-packed earth floor was cleared of accumulated debris. It was hard work, but Naomi was enjoying herself. She liked taking on a battle that she could win.

When she had thoroughly cleaned the inside of the house, she set to work outside, washing the lamp first. After carefully refilling it, she carried it back inside and set it on the brick that extended from the wall for just that purpose.

Jar after jar was then washed and allowed to dry in the sunshine.

While the jars and vessels dried, Naomi sorted bedding, robes, and other clothing. The mats were laid out over bushes and beat briskly with a stick. She left them there to air. She piled the clothing that she would take down to wash and then tied them into a neat bundle that she would carry on her head. By the time she had finished that, the jars were dry, and she carried them back inside.

She glanced around her, trying to decide what to do next. She did not want to leave Cousin Leah outside alone. It was very doubtful that anything would bother her, but she looked so old and helpless lying there asleep that Naomi simply could not leave her. The washing would have to wait.

But she could start on the courtyard. She picked up branches and twigs that had fallen. Then taking the broom, she swept the courtyard clear except around the corner where Cousin Leah slept.

Then she found the mattock and began preparing the small plot of earth that was Cousin Leah's garden. Sweat poured down her face, and her clothing was sticking to her damp body. Often she had to pause and straighten her aching back.

She was thus resting when she saw Ruth walking up the street toward her. She was heavily laden and leading a goat. Gladly, Naomi dropped the mattock and went to meet her.

"What a beautiful goat!" Naomi called to her daughter-in-law, "and your burden is large. You must have traded well indeed!"

Ruth's smile was merry. "Do you think this is a good goat? Why, I assured her former owner that she looked far too young to give good milk, and besides that, her head is too small, and her tail is decidedly crooked!"

They laughed together. "I am glad that I am not trading with you, Ruth. She is a lovely animal, as you well know! Did he trade straight across for the donkey?"

Ruth's smile broadened. "Oh, no, Mother, he also gave me beans and lentils and some gourd seed. Then because she was such a very ugly goat, he added a homer of barley that he will bring later." Ruth laughed in delight at her mother-in-law's expression.

"And what of the other donkey?" Naomi asked in amazement.

"There," Ruth shook her head, "I met my match. That woman was so stiff-necked! Do you know that she accused our lovely donkey of having a crooked foot? And she said he looked old and tired!" She sighed, but her sparkling eyes belied the tone of voice. "So I only have one large cheese, four big loaves of bread, raisins, more lentils, and these coins." She opened her hand to show Naomi the amount of silver that she could have expected to receive for the donkey in full payment.

"Ruth, if you did not have that load on your head, I would hug you! How glad I am that you came with me—and not just because you are such a marvelous trader! God has been good to me to give me a daughter such as you!"

Naomi took the goat's rope, and together they walked toward the courtyard. "I certainly should have had you buy those donkeys in Moab—and deal with Shedeur also. Then perhaps we would have had some silver left when we got here."

They entered the courtyard to find Cousin Leah rousing from sleep. "See what Ruth has brought us! Now we will have milk and cheese," Naomi smiled at Cousin Leah.

"Cousin Leah, who has been bringing your food and caring for you? And why have we not seen anyone here yet?"

"Reuben's daughter Mahlah comes with food for me and to care for my needs when she can get away or does not forget. She came during the morning yesterday. She said they were going to take me to their house within a few days even though they are very crowded. I do not know why she has not come since. It is a wonder that I have not starved; she is so busy with her family."

"Perhaps, she has heard that we are here now and knew that you were being cared for. The whole town seems to have had word of our arrival. But what happened to Reuben?"

"Reuben died two, no, three years ago. And his family has had very little to provide for their own needs. They have done well to feed me the scraps that they did!"

Leah's self-pity irritated Naomi, but she realized that the old woman's neglected condition was partly her responsibility. She had been only too glad to relinquish any care of the crotchety widow to someone else. Now she was back, and the responsibility rested squarely on her shoulders again.

Naomi spoke again, "Cousin Leah, would you like for us to carry you back inside the house now, or would you like to stay out longer?"

After some consideration, Cousin Leah replied, "Oh, let me stay out here for now."

Naomi picked up the bundle of clothes and headed for the troughs where all the village women did their laundry. Tongues normally flew as fast as the hands while they worked. Work became pleasant as they toiled together.

Today the troughs were not crowded—it was much later in the day than women normally did their washing—and Naomi immediately set to work. At first she did not think any of the women there were known to her, but then various ones made themselves known, and soon conversation was lively.

Milkah, Deborah's younger sister, waited for an opening and then began to question Naomi. "Is it true that your daughter-in-law is a Moabite?"

"Yes, Milkah, she is."

"That is so sad," Milkah responded sympathetically. "It must have broken your heart to have your son marry a Moabite!"

"At first I thought so too," Naomi replied. Now all the women were silent. "But Ruth has proved to be a very special blessing. What I would do without her, I do not know!"

"But, Naomi, a heathen girl as part of your family? Elimelech was always so proud of being a Ephrathite, and now you defile the family name by bringing home this Moabite!" Old Dinah was never tactful and was certainly not making this an exception.

"Ruth is no longer a heathen." Naomi struggled to keep the heat out of her voice. "She has chosen our people as her own and now worships the Lord Jehovah as we do—perhaps more faithfully than many of us!"

That silenced her attacker, and Naomi continued. "Ruth is the daughter that I have always wanted. I am very pleased with her. She has been a great comfort and help to me. And she is one of the kindest people I have ever known!"

Some of the women smiled knowingly at one another. They thought that to Naomi, her children had always been the best even though others could easily see that they were no better than average.

But Milkah smiled at Naomi and said, "I am so glad that Ruth has been kind to you. I am eager to meet her. Deborah said that she was friendly and also beautiful."

"Yes, she is lovely in every way, and I praise God for His goodness in giving her to me."

Back in the courtyard she began spreading the clean clothes on bushes. When she returned, she had been surprised to find that Ruth had over half of the garden earth broken up. Now Naomi called to her to stop and rest. But Ruth chose to rest by helping Naomi finish the task of spreading out the clothes to dry.

Then the two of them carried Cousin Leah into the freshly cleaned house. Inside Naomi washed the wrinkled old body gently and then put a fresh tunic and robe on her. By the time she was finished, Cousin Leah was pale with exhaustion, but she did smile her thanks to Naomi before she closed her eyes to rest.

Naomi's heart rejoiced at this first sign that Cousin Leah was softening in her attitude toward her. It was amazing that one smile from the woman she had once despised could mean so much.

But there was still work to be done. She could not sit here dawdling. As she rose, Naomi realized how tired she was, but it was the pleasant tiredness of a day well spent.

She rejoined Ruth in the courtyard. Ruth had started a pot of lentils earlier in the day while Naomi was washing the clothing. With some of the bread and cheese that Ruth had brought home from the market, they would make a delicious meal.

As Naomi and Ruth folded and put away the now dry laundry, Ruth offered a suggestion. "Mother, in the morning I would like to go into the barley fields and glean the dropped ears of grain wherever I can find reapers who will allow me. Please let me go. You know that we will need the grain, and I am strong. I like to work hard." Her speech came out in a rush lest Naomi should say no before she had heard her out.

Naomi did not answer for a moment. Her first inclination was to say no. Ruth was single and a foreigner. It would be risky for her to work in the fields without someone as her protector.

Yet, they would need more food. And this was God's provision for the poor. Some farmers followed the Law and left the corners of their fields for the poor, and most allowed the gleaners to follow behind the reapers and gather the grain the reapers had missed.

Aside from the danger of being accosted, it was back-breaking work with little to show for the hours of labor in the hot sun.

Naomi would rather have gone herself, but she knew that Ruth could endure better than she. And it would be better for Naomi to care for Cousin Leah.

At last Ruth broke the silence. "Please, my mother, let me try—at least one day."

Naomi sighed. Perhaps this, too, was God's provision. She said, "All right, go, my daughter."

When the evening's activities were completed, Naomi was grateful to spread her mat and lie down.

But tired as she was, her mind was busy. She went back over the events of the day, and then turned her thoughts to the Lord. "O my Lord, You have provided for our every need. You have given me work to do and the challenge of winning Cousin Leah over. Thank You, Lord, for these blessings."

13

NAOMI AWOKE WITH FIRST LIGHT. Again, as yesterday, she stepped outside to open the shutters and enjoy the morning. Through the dimness of the dawn she saw the goat. I will milk her right now, she decided. Then when the village girls take out their goats, I will find one to look after ours. She milked the goat dry and carried the vessel of rich milk into the house.

There she found Ruth gathering the foods together for their breakfast. Naomi helped her carry them out. But when they said the blessing and were ready to partake, they found that neither had much appetite. Both were thinking of Ruth's coming venture into the fields, and both were uneasy.

"Ruth, you must eat. You will faint under the heat and toil of the day!" And she cut her daughter-in-law a generous slice of cheese.

Ruth smiled apologetically as she accepted the cheese. "I will try. I know that you are right." She managed to swallow most of the food that Naomi insisted she eat.

As she arose to go to the fields, Naomi quickly wrapped a loaf of bread and a piece of cheese in a scrap of cloth.

"Take this with you, my daughter. You will have to stop to rest during the day, and some food will refresh you."

Naomi walked to the street with her and then kissed her. "May God protect you and give you success, my daughter." She stood watching as Ruth walked toward waiting fields.

After the girl had turned a corner and Naomi could see her no more, she whispered, "O Lord God, the Almighty One, watch over my daughter-in-law. May no harm befall her. And give her strength for the toil of the day."

Her thoughts still with Ruth, Naomi picked up the empty water jar and headed for the well.

While there, she encountered Deborah. They greeted one another cheerfully. How she had missed this friendly contact while she was in Moab!

After chatting about their current activities, Naomi asked her friend's advice. "Deborah, you should be able to help me. We now have a goat, but we have no young girl to send out to the hills with her. Who should I ask to take our goat out with theirs?"

"I certainly can help you. My daughter Zebidah joins the other girls each day in caring for the goats. They go right by Leah's house as they walk out to the hills. I will tell her to stop for your goat."

"Oh, that is wonderful! I will gladly pay her."

"You will not! You have no extra silver to pay for the favors of friends. Let us help you the little that we can."

"Thank you, my friend. You are right, of course, but it is hard to accept the charity of others. I would much rather give."

Deborah gave her an understanding smile and then turned the conversation to other topics.

Upon returning from the well, Naomi found Cousin Leah looking more rested than she had previously. After they had exchanged greetings, Naomi brought her food and helped her eat.

While Cousin Leah was still eating, Zebidah came to pick up Naomi's goat. She and the other girls were in charge of a flock of 10 or 12 goats. They laughed and talked merrily as they led the animals out to the hills. Naomi watched them a moment, remembering the happy days of her childhood.

Then she turned back to the old woman waiting in the house. "Do you ever rise from your mat, Cousin Leah?"

"I have not done so for days. I do not know if I still can." Her voice held the complaint of continual discontent.

"Would you like to try? Perhaps, if you could walk a few steps each day, your strength would return."

"I will try," the old woman decided. "I am tired of lying here, and it was good to be out in the courtyard yesterday," she added with more enthusiasm.

Quickly, Naomi prepared a spot for her to recline when they reached the courtyard. Then she reentered the house to assist her. Getting Cousin Leah up was extremely difficult, and Naomi found herself lifting the frail body with little help from the invalid herself. However, once Cousin Leah was leaning on Naomi for support, she was able to move her feet in a shuffling walk, and huffing and puffing, she managed to move slowly to the courtyard.

The mat and cushions were under a tree, and by grasping a low branch, Cousin Leah was able to partially support her own weight as Naomi carefully lowered her to the resting place. When she was comfortable, Naomi dropped beside her. There passed between them a look of pure triumph. And Naomi thought, This is the first thing that we have done together since we nursed Mahlon and Chilion through their sicknesses so many years ago.

With Cousin Leah settled, Naomi began her grinding. Today she would make flour. Then she would make it into bread and take it to the village oven to bake.

As she settled into grinding, Naomi found pleasure in the soothing hum of the millstones. The turning of the top stone kept her hands busy, but it left her mind free. Determinedly, she kept her thoughts on household matters. How I would have scorned barley bread just a few years ago! I would not have considered grinding anything but wheat to feed my family. But the Lord has taught me much, and my heart is truly thankful for this barley.

She stopped turning the stone to pour more grain through the central hole. Quickly regaining the rhythmic turning of the stone, she lifted her heart in song. "I will sing to the Lord for He is highly exalted; . . . The Lord is my strength and My song, And He has become my salvation; This is my God, and I will praise Him."

With a spirit of praise she continued on through the triumphant song of Moses. As she reached the words, "In Thy lovingkindness Thou hast led the people whom Thou hast redeemed," her joyful heart cried, "O Lord, that fits me. You have redeemed me from my sinful, wayward self, and You have led me back to Your land!" Tears of joy stained her face.

As she stopped again to add grain, she discovered Cousin Leah watching her skeptically. "And what do you have to be so happy about? It seems to me that you should be mourning in sackcloth and ashes and begging the Lord to have mercy upon you. Has His chastisement not even touched your hard heart?"

Her attack took Naomi by surprise, but after a moment she answered, "I have mourned the deaths of my loved ones and my own sinfulness. But now I rejoice because God has heard me. He has forgiven my sins and brought me back to my homeland. Like Job, 'I know that my Redeemer lives, And at the last He will take His stand on the earth.' My joy is in the Lord, not in myself."

"Humph! You always were a strange person!" And with that the old woman settled herself more comfortably with her face turned away from Naomi.

After finishing the grinding, Naomi mixed her bread. "Cousin Leah," she touched the woman's shoulder as she spoke, and when she awakened, asked her, "will you be all right while I go to bake our bread?"

"Yes, of course. I managed for 10 years without you."

Not knowing how to respond, Naomi replied, "I will be back as quickly as I can," and hurriedly left the courtyard.

As she walked, she considered the other work that was pressing. The rest of the garden must be turned, and the seeds planted as quickly as possible.

Then her thoughts turned to the ever-present concern. I wonder how Ruth is getting along. The day is getting very warm. Will it be too much for her? Is she being treated well? "O Lord, will You please protect her?"

At the oven Naomi waited her turn to put her bread into the huge vault. As the women waited, they talked. Many wanted to hear Naomi's story, so she faced a barrage of questions. It was trying for her to retell her sad tale, but she knew that in time relief would come; the curious would shift their attention to someone else.

At last her bread was baked, and she hurried home with the aromatic loaves. The heat was now intense, and by the time she reached the shade of the courtyard, she was ready to rest.

Naomi slept and awoke in midafternoon, feeling sluggish from the heat. But she arose and started working resolutely in the garden. Her muscles complained as she began to wield the mattock, but gradually they eased as she continued. And as she worked, the natural rhythm of chopping with the mattock returned to her. She kept her eyes on the unturned earth, watching the plot grow smaller and smaller. At last she finished and straightened with some difficulty. She glanced at the sun, now far down in the western sky. She must quickly get the jar and go for water. Ruth would enjoy a cold drink when she returned from the fields. And no doubt, she would want a bath. And I could use one too! Naomi thought as she shook her damp clothing loose from her body and started for the well.

When Naomi returned, everything seemed to need doing at once. Cousin Leah was hungry and wanted to return to her mat inside. Zebidah and the other girls returned with the goats just as Naomi was preparing to move Cousin Leah.

Before long things had been resolved. Another of the girls tethered Naomi's goat while Zebidah helped Naomi move Cousin Leah inside. Then the girls went on to their own homes, still carefree and gay after their day in the hills. Naomi took food to the old cousin and saw that she was comfortable. Then she was able to milk the goat without interruption.

As she milked, her thoughts were anxious. The worries that she had pushed aside during the day now crowded in. Surely Ruth should be here soon! What if she did not come? What if she could not? Naomi had fully expected the Moabite girl to receive verbal abuse, but would the Israelite men do her physical harm as well?

Stop it! she admonished herself fiercely. You are imagining all of this. She will be here soon.

And Ruth did come soon, just before the sun dropped out of sight in the west. Naomi spotted her coming some distance down the street and hurried out to meet her. "Ruth, is it well with you, my daughter? My, what a load you have!"

"Yes, Mother, I am well. And just wait until you see what my bundle contains!"

They entered the courtyard, and Ruth opened her bundle. About an ephah of barley grain lay in the cloth. While Naomi stood in open-mouthed surprise, Ruth took some roasted grain from her pocket and gave it to her mother-in-law. "Here, this is for your supper. I had more than I could eat."

"But how, why, . . . Where did you glean today? May the one who took notice of you be blessed of the Lord!"

"Come, my mother, let us eat. I am as hungry as a starving camel. I will tell you all about it. Oh, you baked fresh bread today! It smells so good."

As soon as Naomi had offered thanks, Ruth began eating with a healthy appetite. Naomi, not nearly as hungry as she was curious to hear her daughter-in-law's tale, watched in amusement.

At last Ruth's appetite was sated, and she met her mother-in-law's gaze with an answering smile.

"Now tell me," Naomi demanded, "in whose field did you glean today?"

"The name of the man with whom I worked today is Boaz . . ."

"May he be blessed of the Lord!" Naomi interrupted. "Indeed the Lord has not withdrawn His kindness to the living and to the dead. Boaz is one of our closest relatives; he is Elimelech's kinsman.

"But I interrupted you. Tell me all about your day, my daughter."

"Well, as I went this morning, I asked the Lord God to guide me. I came to a field where the reapers were busy. After gaining permission, I began to glean after them.

"Sometime later I glanced up to see an important looking man enter the field. He greeted the reapers, saying, 'May the Lord be with you.'

"And they answered him, 'May the Lord bless you.'

"Then I heard him ask, 'Whose young woman is this?'

"You can imagine how my heart stood still. I did not think they could know who I was, but I was surprised to hear one of the reapers reply, 'She is the young Moabite who returned with Naomi from the land of Moab. She asked for permission to glean among the reapers and among the sheaves, and it was granted. She has been here working since morning with only a brief rest.'

"I hardly breathed while he spoke, and I was even more frightened when I saw Boaz draw that servant away and speak with him so that I could not hear. I thought my heart would stop when I saw Boaz heading toward me. But his manner was kind, and I lost most of my fear even before he spoke. He has such a gentle face! Then he said, 'Listen carefully, my daughter. Do not go to glean in another field; be sure you do not go from this one, but stay here with my maidservants. Watch which field they reap, and follow them all through the harvest. Indeed, I have commanded the servants not to touch you. And when you are thirsty, go to the water jars and drink from what the servants have drawn.'

"I fell down before him with my face to the ground to thank him. But I could not resist asking, 'Why have I found favor in your sight that you should take notice of me, a foreigner?'

"And do you know what he said? He said that he had heard that I had been kind to you since Mahlon's death." Ruth's voice was full of awe that the great man had been impressed by the story he had heard of her. She continued, "He said he had had a full report, and that he knew I had left my own parents and my homeland to come to live among a people that I did not know.

"And then he blessed me, saying, 'May the Lord reward your work, and may your wages be full from the Lord, the God of Israel, under whose wings you have come to seek refuge.'

"I was so amazed! I took courage to answer him, 'I have found favor in your sight, my lord, for you have comforted me and have spoken kindly to me, your maidservant, although I am so different from your own maidservants.'"

She stopped her recital to draw a deep breath. Naomi's heart was full of thankfulness. She reached over and patted Ruth's hand.

"Then," Ruth continued, "at mealtime Boaz again spoke to me. He urged me to come to the table with his reapers and to dip my bread in the wine. He served me the roasted grain that they were eating. I ate what I could, but I had this left that I have brought to you. Actually, I could eat very little; I was so excited. Before the others were finished, I left the table to go back to gleaning.

"This afternoon I found much more grain left behind the reapers than I did this morning. I was amazed to see how much grain I had after I had threshed it out."

"Boaz has cared for you well, my daughter. It is good that you should stay with his maidservants lest others should accost you in another field.

"All through the day I have been concerned about you," Naomi smiled, remembering her fears, "but the Lord God has used Boaz to provide for you and to protect you. Truly the Lord is to be praised!"

Later that night when Naomi had settled herself for sleep, she found her mind full of an idea that had come to her as Ruth had reported the day's happenings.

But I must not run ahead of the Lord, she told herself. I have caused so much trouble by being sure that I knew what was best for everyone.

"O Lord God of my fathers, I thank You for Your provision and for protecting Ruth. I ask Your leading regarding the future. May Your will be done."

14

*A*S THE DAYS PASSED, a routine developed in the household of Cousin Leah, Naomi, and Ruth. Early each morning Ruth left for the fields of Boaz. Naomi made Cousin Leah comfortable, either in the house or in the courtyard, whichever Leah preferred on that particular day. Then Naomi set about her own work of getting water, grinding meal, cooking, or laundry. Some days she was able to do some weaving, and idle moments were filled with spinning.

The garden had been planted, and the plants were growing sturdily. Naomi never tired of the wonder of growing things, whether it be plant or animal.

During the hottest part of the day, Naomi lay down to rest as did almost the entire population of Bethlehem. In the cooler months, one could continue to work during midday, but in the heat of summer, it was almost impossible.

Each evening Ruth came home from the fields, bearing a generous bundle of grain. She was tired but cheerful after her day's work. Her body was young and healthy, and work was no hardship to her. If the day had been particularly hot, her exhaustion was obvious in the way she moved, but never did Naomi hear the girl complain.

In fact, as the days passed, Ruth became lighter of heart. Her eyes sparkled gaily; her lips curved into a smile most of the time, and the courtyard often rang with her laughter.

Surely, the move to Israel had been right for Ruth. Naomi just hoped that Orpah was well and happy back in Moab. She felt that she had failed Orpah. So she prayed frequently for her and tried to leave her in the strong hands of her loving God.

Each evening, Naomi and Ruth discussed their day's activities, and Naomi began to suspect that Boaz was the reason behind Ruth's increased happiness. Ruth did not often mention his name, however, and when she did, it was only to praise his kindness. But her glowing face revealed her inner thoughts even though her words did not.

Occasionally Naomi would speak of Boaz or ask Ruth about him just to watch the girl's reaction. And all the while, the seed of her idea grew.

One evening, after Ruth had again mentioned Boaz's generosity, Naomi told her of his past. "Boaz has always been kind, even from his youth. Although his father, Salmon, was probably the wealthiest man in Bethlehem, Boaz never allowed his riches to affect his attitude toward others. From the poorest child to the wealthy ones, all were his friends.

"He was only a few years younger than I, and I remember him as a merry boy. Only once did I see him become really angry."

Ruth was listening intently as Naomi continued the story. "A group of boys had captured a young hawk and were mistreating him. They baited him with sticks, and then when he finally refused to attack a stick, they began throwing stones at him—all this while the poor bird was tethered to a sapling with a leather thong.

"I had been trying my best to rescue the bird, but they were so many, and they just laughed at my efforts.

"That is when Boaz appeared, attracted, he told me later, by my screams of rage. Taking in the situation at a glance, he promptly flew at those boys—all of them larger than he. It must have been the shock of seeing the gentle Boaz in a fury that stopped them. At any rate, they withdrew shamefaced, and he and I managed to loose the hawk.

"It was too late, of course. In spite of our best care, the bird died. Boaz wept with me as we buried him and erected a cairn of stones above the little grave."

Ruth's face reflected both sadness and then pride as Naomi progressed through the story. "He truly is a kind and gentle person," she said softly when Naomi had finished.

"I wonder if, perhaps, he learned his compassion from sad experiences," Naomi mused. "His mother Rahab was a harlot from Jericho. But she turned to the Lord God, and when Joshua sent spies into Jericho before attacking the city, she protected them at the risk of her own life. In return, when the city fell, Joshua instructed the spies to rescue her and her family. They were taken back to live just outside the camp of Israel.

"Then Salmon married Rahab, and she became one of our people. But some still treated her with contempt, remembering what she had been. I am sure that Boaz must have witnessed her misery. I think that may be why he is so concerned over those who are mistreated, whether animal or human."

"Like me," Ruth smiled. "He has certainly made sure that I do not suffer any ill treatment."

"Yes, he has been very kind to both of us. Deborah tells me that he has recently suffered great sorrow himself. He married about the time we left for Moab. But his wife was never able to bear him living children. Then just a year ago, she died after several years of illness, leaving him alone. My heart aches for his sadness. I think it is even more difficult for a man to be left alone than it is for a woman."

Tears of sympathy glistened in Ruth's eyes, and she

only nodded in reply. Naomi could see that she shared Boaz's grief, and she again felt a surge of hope that her plan might be workable. But she knew that she must bide her time.

Barley harvest ended, but wheat harvest followed immediately, so there was no break in the routine. Only now the grain that Ruth brought home was wheat, and once again Naomi could make the delicious wheat bread that she had made in the past. How Cousin Leah enjoyed the treat! Many years had passed since those who cared for her had been able to afford wheat flour.

But the days did not bring only happy thoughts. As Naomi joyfully watched Ruth become increasingly happy, she also watched Cousin Leah fail. Daily she seemed to have less strength.

Her appetite dwindled, and even the fresh cucumbers from the garden could not tempt her. Naomi tried every food that she could think of—all to no avail. Cousin Leah would swallow a few bites and then refuse more nourishment.

Wherever she lay, Cousin Leah spent most of her time asleep. When she did awaken, she lay unmoving, seemingly uncaring, until she again fell asleep. Naomi tried to break through the apathy, but she had no success.

One day, when Naomi was at her wit's end trying to persuade the old woman to eat, she burst out, "Cousin Leah, you must eat! If you do not, you will just wither away and die!" And Naomi began to cry.

For once Cousin Leah's eyes regained their snap. "And why should that matter? I am an old woman. I have seen enough of trouble and sorrow. Let me die in peace."

Naomi had turned her head away, trying to hide her tears from the invalid while fighting for control. Then she felt Cousin Leah's hand on her arm. "You really do care!" The tired old voice held wonder. "Do not cry, my daughter. I know that you have seen too much of death, but it holds no horror for me. I am ready to be laid with my fathers. Do not grieve for me."

Naomi bent and gathered Cousin Leah into her arms in a warm embrace. Her wet cheek lay against the dry, withered face. And the warmth of peace spread through her as Cousin Leah patted her back.

Moments later, both women felt awkward and constrained. Any tenderness between them was a new and fragile shoot to be nurtured with great care, not to be commented upon hastily.

It was two days later, early in the morning when her strength was at its peak, that Cousin Leah again broached the subject of her death. "Naomi, after I die, you are to keep this house. There is no one who has any more right to it than you, and I want you to have it." She paused and then continued with difficulty, "You have been kind to a cranky old woman. Your goodness in these last days has overshadowed any unkindness you were guilty of in the past. You have matured into a good woman."

"Oh, Cousin Leah, thank you for your kindness. I will be honored to accept your house as my own after you sleep with your fathers—may that be many days hence! But it is not just that I have grown up. God has been shaping my life. To Him be the glory for any kindness He has put within me."

Cousin Leah just shook her head weakly, saying, "As you wish," and closed her eyes as if to sleep.

Fearfully, Naomi watched over her that day. Somehow the old cousin looked different, but Naomi could not pin down the difference or find any specific cause for alarm.

But when she awoke the next morning, it was to find Cousin Leah's body lifeless. The old woman had died quietly in her sleep.

Although Naomi had been expecting the death at any time, it came as a grim shock. With heart knotted tight in her chest, Naomi awoke Ruth and sent her to alert Mahlah and the others of Reuben's family. Just before she let her out the door, she added, "And come back by Caleb's house and tell Deborah."

Alone in the room with the corpse, Naomi began the death wail, crying out, "Ah, my mother! Alas, my beloved!"

Quickly, the neighbors began to gather, and soon Ruth was back, bringing Reuben's daughter Mahlah and also Deborah. Many other mourners followed them. Together the women washed the frail old body and wrapped it for burial, and all the while the house rang with the combined wailing of the mourners.

Some of the men had gone immediately to dig a grave not far outside the village. When they returned, the lifeless body was placed on a bier, and four men carried it off. The mourners followed, and their wails echoed eerily through the streets as they passed.

After Cousin Leah's body had been buried, the sad procession made its way back to the house, still wailing. But now sorrow must begin to give way to practical considerations. Food must be set out for the mourners. Ruth and Naomi worked together in quiet harmony, preparing the food. Mahlah and Deborah both brought bread and wine from their own houses, and with what Naomi had on hand, it was enough. The mourning would continue for two more days, but those who mourned would help to provide the food. And Naomi was thankful to have familiar work to put her hand to.

As she surveyed the crowd gathered in the courtyard, Naomi reflected, This is the first time that I have appreciated the mourners who wept with me. When my father died, I was so shocked and angry that I wanted to share my sorrow with no one. I am sure that the healing would have come more quickly if I had been willing to be comforted by others who grieved also. But I would not.

And when my dear Elimelech and my sons died, I was among strangers. Their customs were similar, but they did not share my sorrow, and I could not bear to hire heathen Moabites to mourn my Israelite husband and sons.

But this is as it should be. Cousin Leah was ready for her life to be over, and I am surrounded by friends who loved her and who care about me.

And so Naomi was comforted in the loss of the woman whom once she had despised but recently had come to love.

It was the fourth day after Cousin Leah's death that Ruth went back to the fields of Boaz. Naomi had dreaded this lonely day and yet also looked forward to a time to be alone. She felt in great need of respite from the constant company of those who had surrounded her the last few days.

For months after Elimelech's death she had found herself listening for his footsteps as evening approached. And the horror of turning over in her sleep to touch him and to find herself alone, still turned a knife in her heart.

And her sons—how often she still heard a deep masculine voice or sensed someone near and looked up, expecting to see Mahlon or Chilion. Each time it happened, it was as if their death was a fresh wound.

Deborah must have understood her friend's loneliness. She came over during the morning and sat opposite Naomi at the millstones. As they worked together, turning the stone, Naomi was able to share some of her feelings with her friend. "It is not as though Cousin Leah and I were ever really close. I know people may even think my grief a sham, but I did come to love her. Many times each day, especially at the last, she needed me to move her or make her more comfortable. Everything I did was planned around her needs. Now my day seems empty without her."

"I will not say that I understand just how you feel," Deborah replied. "I am sure that I do not. But I do know what sorrow means. I lost a little daughter just five years ago. She was not like other children, even as a baby. She was unusually small and never grew properly. And she seemed to be in great pain much of the time. The only way that I could soothe her was to hold her in my arms. Day after day I sat wrapped in the needs of my tiny daughter. Often I cried, both for her pain and for my own frustration. The rest of my family suffered; I had no time to care for my house or my family as I should.

"But then she died, and my world fell apart. It took some time and the wisdom of my mother to show me that Caleb and my other children needed me badly—that I must begin to make up to them for the hours of neglect. I still miss my baby, but now my days are full once more, and I rejoice in caring for all my family."

Naomi stopped the millstone and wiped her eyes. "Thank you for sharing that with me, Deborah. I never knew. Indeed, I had begun to think that I alone had suffered. I am so glad that you told me!"

They resumed the grinding, and when Deborah left at midday, Naomi felt greatly comforted.

The day was very hot. Gratefully, Naomi entered the slightly cooler house for a rest. She knew that even the field servants of Boaz would be resting now. Boaz never mistreated his servants, Ruth reported. So Naomi lay down, knowing that Ruth, also, was resting.

As she lay there, her mind was busy. Could I make provision so that Ruth would be cared for? And so that a child might be raised up in Mahlon's name? But I must not rush into this. I could cause Ruth much anguish if it did not work out.

And do I really want only what is best for Ruth? Or am I again thinking of myself and what I want?

"O Lord God of Israel, guide me. Let me not fail Ruth. Let me know Your way.

"O my Lord, I claim the promise that Moses gave to Your people Israel, 'Be strong and courageous, do not be afraid or tremble at them, for the Lord your God is the one who goes with you. He will not fail you or forsake you.'"

15

▼▲▼▲▼▲▼

*T*HE LONG, HOT DAYS of wheat harvest were nearly finished. The reapers longed for the last field to be completed. All of them, that is, but the gleaner from Moab.

Ruth did not seem to suffer from the heat as much as some did. Ruth seemed to endure the heat in the fields better than Naomi could in the relative coolness of the shady courtyard.

But Ruth's hardiness was not the reason she did not long for the end of harvest with the others, Naomi was sure. The closer they drew to the end of harvest, the quieter Ruth became.

One evening, Naomi said, "Your gleaning has been of great benefit, my daughter. Due to your work and Boaz's generosity, we have enough barley and wheat to last all year. The garden is doing well also. We may not eat like princes, but we should certainly have plenty."

"Yes, it is good to have provisions for the winter." But Ruth's face did not brighten.

No, Naomi thought, it was not concern for their grain supply that was the problem. And sure that she did know the true reason behind Ruth's low spirits, Naomi turned her mind to her plan with fresh enthusiasm.

Now Naomi was as eager as Ruth was reluctant for the harvest to be finished. Only when harvest was over would she put the plan into action.

Her plan involved some risk to Ruth, to her pride, if not to her person. But Naomi was eager to set it in motion and eager to know the outcome.

At last, the day came. Ruth arrived home in midafternoon, rather than just before sunset as was usual. With her, she carried the last of the wheat that she had gleaned from Boaz's fields.

Upon hearing the girl's step, Naomi glanced up from her spinning. "Ah, Ruth, you are finished at last!" She smiled cheerfully.

"Yes, the gleaning is done for this year." Ruth paused, and hurriedly added, "But, Mother, would it not be well for me to seek a position as a servant now? That would keep me from being a burden to you. And," she rushed on, "I would rather work hard than sit idle day after day. Oh, I know I could help you grind and spin, but there will not be enough work to keep us both busy this winter. I think Boaz might hire me to work with his maidservants; he has spoken well of my work."

"No, my daughter. That will not do. But sit down here beside me." Naomi continued, "I have considered the matter carefully. You shall not be a servant but a bride, if we can but arrange it."

Seeing Ruth's amazement, she went on, "Should I not seek marriage for you, that it may be well with you?

"You remember, my dear, God's provision that a brother should marry the childless widow to raise up a child to carry on the name of the dead husband. Of course, Mahlon's brother is also dead, but a near kinsman is then responsible to take the brother's place.

"And Boaz, who has shown you such great kindness and has carefully protected you, is our near kinsman. It is my plan that he should become your goel.

"Tonight he will be winnowing barley at the threshing floor. This is what you must do. Bathe and anoint your body with perfume. Dress in your best clothes. Then you must go down to the threshing floor. You will go in after dark so that no one will recognize you."

Naomi hurried on with the instructions lest Ruth voice her reluctance. "After he has eaten his bread and drunk his wine, he will lie down on the threshing floor to guard his grain. Watch where he lies down, and then go very quietly, uncover his feet, and lie down at his feet. Do nothing more until he tells you what to do.

"This will let him know that you are willing for him to become your kinsman-redeemer. Then the decision is up to him.

"Boaz is an honorable man. He will not treat you with disrespect; you will be as safe with him as if you were here with me. And, perhaps, he will be willing to marry you."

She looked at Ruth's now downcast face and added, "You could confront him publicly, but that would cause both of you humiliation if he should not choose to redeem you."

Finally, Naomi stopped speaking and watched Ruth closely. At last she looked up, and her expression was a mixture of hope and fear. Her answer was quiet but firm. "All that you say, I will do." And she arose to begin her bath.

Sometime later, when Ruth was groomed and dressed, she stood before Naomi for approval. "You look lovely, my daughter. I pray that God will grant you a husband and children.

"Now go. Keep the veil about your face so that none can recognize you. May the Lord watch over you, my daughter."

After Ruth had slipped out of sight, Naomi sat in the

darkness of the courtyard. Her hands trembled. The plan was in action, and right or wrong, Ruth was on her way.

Naomi trusted Ruth to follow her instructions implicitly, but what if something unforeseen came up?

She gave herself a mental shake. Stop it! You must just trust her to the Lord. He can care for her in the dark of night as well as in the light of day.

After a time, Naomi forced herself to enter the silent house and lie down upon her mat. Whether I sleep or not, she thought, I will lie here and try to rest. Everything is in the hands of Ruth and Boaz—and in the mighty hands of the Lord God—especially in the hands of the Lord God.

Naomi realized that she must have slept, for she was suddenly aware that the moon shone brightly. She could see the light around the shutters. She arose and walked out into the courtyard. She felt wide awake, completely alert. Perhaps, if I do not try to sleep for a time, I will be able to relax and rest later, she thought.

But what should I do? I dare not grind. The noise of the millstones could be heard by the neighbors. They would certainly wonder about it and perhaps ask questions.

Then she spied the spindle lying in the basket of wool. I could spin by moonlight. Even blind old women could spin, so I certainly could do it in the semidarkness of this moonlit night. As she worked, she realized how little one used eyesight in spinning. It was the work of the fingers to determine the thickness of the thread.

And the work was soothing. Her busy fingers and the repetition of movement brought relaxation.

A good part of the wool had become thread on the spindle when, at last, Naomi became drowsy and left the spinning to return to her mat.

She awoke just before daylight. She lay tense and still, trying to remember what had awakened her. Then she saw the door was open.

She sat up and saw a figure moving in the house. "Ruth?" And as the girl turned suddenly, she cried, "Oh, Ruth, how did it go, my daughter?"

After that first jump of surprise, Ruth had stood silently with hands pressed hard against her wildly thumping heart. "Oh, my mother, how you startled me!" Then she added, "It went well, I think. I am not sure yet."

Not sure? What had gone wrong? She had thought that it would be decided, one way or the other, by now. Naomi felt a knot of fear tighten in her chest, but with great effort, she kept her words calm. "Come, tell me."

Ruth sat down beside her and began her story. "I did just as you instructed me. I was careful to keep my eyes lowered and my veil close around my face as I walked out to the threshing floor. It bothered me that those who saw me assumed me to be a harlot seeking business among the men. However, no one spoke to me or troubled me.

"When I arrived at the threshing floor, I could see the men eating their supper and drinking the wine, so I hid myself in the shadows and waited. Boaz even stands out among the men as a great and good man!" she added with pride.

Then Ruth's face clouded, "But, my mother, as I stood there watching, a question came to me. You told Orpah and me once that it was wrong for Mahlon and Chilion to marry us because we were foreign women. You said that God had promised to destroy His people who intermarried with foreigners. And Mahlon and Chilion are dead! Is it right for Boaz to marry me now? Will God destroy him also? I know that his mother was a foreigner, but does that make a difference? I would not want to bring him harm!"

Naomi patted her hand reassuringly. "It was indeed wrong for Mahlon to marry you when you were a foreigner. But, my daughter, you are no longer a foreigner. Your family may be of Moab, but your heart became Israelite when you chose the people of Israel as your own and turned to the true God. You need have no fear that Boaz will suffer from marrying a Moabite."

"I was truly worried and afraid," Ruth confessed. "But I thought that, somehow, it must be all right because you had told me clearly what to do. I decided that I must just obey your directions and do as you had said. I am glad that I am no longer a foreigner," she added with a relieved smile.

Then, sensing Naomi's impatience to hear the rest of the story, she continued, "By the time Boaz had laid down by his pile of grain, I was shaking from head to foot. Finally, I thought he would be asleep, and I crept over to where he lay. I carefully laid aside his robe off his feet." She giggled now, remembering her terror lest Boaz should awaken right then and demand to know what she was doing.

"Then," she continued, "I lay down *very* carefully, right at his feet. I thought that I would never sleep as I lay there, but I did! The next thing I knew, Boaz was sitting up and speaking to me. Oh, how I jumped then! And for a moment my wits seemed to have forsaken me.

"I am sure that Boaz was as startled as I. He asked a second time, 'Who are you?' before I could find my voice to answer him.

"At last I said, 'I am Ruth, your maid. Please spread your covering over your maid, for you are a near kinsman.'

"For a moment he did not reply, and I trembled. But when he spoke, his voice was gentle. 'May you be blessed of the Lord, my daughter. You have shown even more kindness than you did earlier because you have not sought a young husband, rich or poor. You have chosen to seek a kinsman redeemer as our Law teaches.

"'Do not fear, my daughter'—he must have sensed my shaking—'I will be honored to do as you ask. Indeed, all the city realizes what an excellent woman you are!

"'But there is a problem.' My heart sank at his words! 'It is true that I am a near kinsman, but there is a relative closer than I. He has first claim.

" 'But you stay here tonight, and tomorrow I will consult with him. If he wants to redeem you, then you must marry him. But if he does not wish to redeem you, then I will marry you. As the Lord lives, I give you my pledge. So lie down now and rest until the morning.'

"And he spread his cloak over me and then lay back down himself. And throughout the night it was as though there was a wall between us. He acted as though I were not there. He did not touch me." Ruth's voice held wonder at the restraint Boaz had shown and the respectful manner in which he had treated her.

"He lay so still, and his breathing was not deep and even as of one sleeping. I knew that he lay there as wakeful as I. Eventually, I slept again, but I do not think that he did. At any rate, he awakened me while it was still very dark. He told me that I must leave lest anyone know I had been there.

"Then he had me take off my cloak, and he poured into it six measures of barley. He bundled it up and put it on my head and told me to bring it to you. He said, 'Do not go to your mother-in-law empty-handed.'

"So here I am. I did not meet anyone as I returned, and the grain is there in the corner. Now I do not know whether to laugh or cry. It appears that I will be a bride again as you promised, but I do not know who my bridegroom will be."

Naomi gave her daughter-in-law a troubled smile in the early morning light. "I had forgotten about Ahira," Naomi admitted with a sigh. "He is not so rich as Boaz, but that is not the reason that I hope he will not want to redeem you." She hesitated to consider her words before adding simply, "He already has one wife."

Although Naomi would not allow herself to frighten Ruth by telling her just what Ahira's wife was like, her tone of voice conveyed to Ruth a great deal of what was in her thoughts. But Ruth remained silent regarding her own fears, and Naomi quickly changed the subject.

"Just wait, my daughter," she said encouragingly. "Boaz will not rest until he has settled it today. Before the sun sets, you should know what is to happen.

"But as you wait," she added more cheerfully, "it would be well to pray. I know that you have a preference in the matter, and so do I. The Lord God knows all things. I know He will give you what is best. But let us ask Him right now."

With her arm around Ruth's shoulders, Naomi stood before the Lord. "O God of my fathers," Naomi prayed, "we thank You for Boaz's kindness and his willingness to be goel for Ruth. O Almighty One, would You intervene that he might be Ruth's husband rather than Ahira whom she does not know? O Lord, I would that Ruth should be Boaz's only and cherished wife, rather than a second wife in the house of Ahira. But we leave it in Your hands."

16

▼▼▼▼▼▼▼▼

NAOMI AND RUTH WEARILY STARTED the routine work of the day. But while their bodies felt the strain, their minds were active and alert.

What would Boaz find out? Would Ahira want Ruth as a second wife? And even if he did not, would he accept her in order to gain the land of Elimelech that was tied into the bargain?

As Naomi watched, she could almost read her daughter-in-law's thoughts from the expressions crossing the girl's face. Now a fleeting smile—surely caused by a memory of an act or word of Boaz; then an anxious biting of the lips— what has she heard of Ahira to cause her to fear him? Naomi wondered.

After a time, Naomi began to sing the song that Moses sang to Israel not long before his death.

> *Give ear, O heavens, and let me speak;*
> *And let the earth hear the words of my mouth.*
> *Let my teaching drop as the rain,*
> *My speech distill as the dew,*
> *As the droplets on the fresh grass*

And as the showers on the herb.
For I proclaim the name of the Lord;
Ascribe greatness to our God!
The Rock! His work is perfect,
For all His ways are just;
A God of faithfulness and without injustice,
Righteous and upright is He.

As Naomi sang, her heart rose in praise to the Lord. Truly, He is a "God of faithfulness." On and on through the song, she continued, and as she recounted God's care for His people, she felt confident that He would also care for Ruth and herself with great kindness.

Ruth seemed cheered by the words of praise. When Naomi stopped singing, she said wistfully, "I wish I knew the songs of praise that you know. Would you teach me?"

Delighted, Naomi agreed quickly. "Yes, my daughter. Let us start right now."

So they started again at the beginning of the song, with Naomi singing a phrase and Ruth repeating it like an echo. This was even better for keeping their minds busy, and the morning passed quickly.

The two women had just finished their grinding when Boaz appeared, walking down the street to their courtyard. Naomi had not yet seen him when she looked up and saw Ruth's face. Then she turned quickly to see Boaz striding purposefully toward them.

Both women arose and bowed low as he entered the courtyard.

"Peace be on you, my lord."

"And on you peace. I bring tidings that I trust will give you joy. Ahira has relinquished his right to Elimelech's property and to his daughter-in-law. He felt that he would endanger his own inheritance for his children were he to become goel." Boaz hastened to add the excuse for his relative, lest Ruth should feel herself personally rejected.

"So now the way stands clear for me to buy the property and to take Ruth as my wife. You should know that I am delighted with his decision. I think that he must surely have never seen Ruth, or he would not have decided thus." He smiled at the blushing girl.

"And now we must plan for the future. Surely there is no need for a long betrothal?" He looked to Naomi for her response. "When may I take Ruth to my house as my wife?"

Naomi's heart was so full of joy it was difficult to speak. But once the words came, they bubbled like a rippling brook. "Oh, my lord, this is wonderful! God has answered my prayers. I know that you will care well for my daughter and give her joy. But we must have a few days to prepare Ruth to become your bride. Perhaps one week would seem fitting to you?"

"It is well. I have already made the legal arrangements to buy the land of Elimelech and keep it in trust for the first son of Ruth. Now I will go and see that my house is ready for the wedding feast. I will come in one week to take my bride to my house. And you, my sister, will also be an honored part of my household," he added.

Naomi hesitated. She had been sure that this would arise, but she did not want to go to the house of Boaz just yet. She would like to give Ruth some time as his wife before she moved in.

"Would it be seemly, my lord, if I were to tarry here until after the Feast of Tabernacles? I promised Elimelech that I would go to Shiloh and offer sacrifices after I returned to Israel. I would want to fulfill my promise to him before I began a new life of comfort and ease in your house."

She thought that Boaz might argue that it was a lame excuse, but his answer was kindly. "It will be as you wish, but you must not remain here after the rains begin. I think your roof must leak badly. And any time before that, if you wish to come, you are welcome in my house."

Then he spoke directly to Ruth for the first time since his arrival. "Ruth, you are a woman to be praised. I am honored to redeem you and make you my wife."

Ruth's face remained modestly lowered, but she smiled even as the blush again spread over her face.

Boaz turned once again to Naomi. "With your permission, I will depart."

"Depart in peace," she responded, and then stood watching him as he walked down the narrow street.

When Boaz was out of sight, Naomi turned and hugged Ruth enthusiastically. "It is done!" she cried. "You will be secure and at peace among the people of Israel. God has rewarded your kindness to me—but Ruth! Are you crying? Is not this pleasing to you?"

"Oh, my mother," Ruth sobbed. "I am crying because my heart is overflowing. Truly the Lord has blessed his handmaid! My soul is full of praise to Him!" And she clung to her mother-in-law while the tears streamed down her cheeks.

"And you are very tired," Naomi observed. "You have been working hard in the fields and have been under considerable strain for many weeks. Now that things are settled, your body and emotions are worn out. You rest now while the sun is too hot for work. Perhaps you will sleep and then will feel refreshed."

She led the weeping girl into the slightly cooler house and quickly unrolled her mat. When Ruth had lain down, Naomi spread her own mat and reclined also. She, too, was weary.

When Naomi awoke some time later, Ruth slept on. The older woman went about her work quietly. Ruth is truly exhausted, she thought. The extra rest will do her good. Perhaps she might even sleep through the night.

When evening drew near and Naomi left for the well, Ruth still slept. The day had begun to cool, and the air was comfortable as Naomi walked down the narrow street. How marvelous everything seems this afternoon! Naomi thought. Our future is secure. I am among my own people. And best of all, God seems to be showing His favor by blessing me, His servant. Truly I am back in the "place of blessing"!

At the well the women's chatter seemed louder and more excited than usual. But when Naomi appeared, there was a momentary lull, and then the voices and the questions all seemed to be aimed at her.

"Is it true that Boaz is becoming goel for Ruth?"

"How fortunate you are! Now you will be a part of a really wealthy household."

"Like father, like son! They seem to have a taste for foreign women," an old woman's voice cackled with coarse laughter.

Then Deborah was beside Naomi. "Hush," she commanded the noisy, crowding women. "Let Naomi speak. She will tell you the true story."

Naomi smiled her thanks to her friend, and then spoke. "Yes, it is true that Ruth and Boaz are betrothed. As you know, he is a near relative of my husband Elimelech, and he has become her kinsman-redeemer, her goel. I am sure that you will all be invited to the wedding feast."

Another questioner broke in, "But what of Ahira? I was sure that he would want the land of Elimelech to farm with his own." Her tone implied that somehow Ahira was being deprived of his rights.

Naomi answered the question and the innuendo quietly. "He did not wish to endanger his own children's inheritance by buying Elimelech's land and taking Ruth as a wife. It has been settled between them that Boaz should become the goel."

"Yes," Deborah broke in, "Caleb was a witness to the agreement this morning. It is done."

The women continued to buzz around Naomi, many of them rejoicing with her. But a few seemed resentful and jealous of her new status. Naomi was sure that they thought she did not deserve such bounty from the Lord, and she knew that she truly did not. But God had blessed, and she accepted His gifts gratefully.

When Naomi left the well, Deborah walked with her. "Caleb and I are so happy that things have worked out well for you," and her beaming face was evidence of her joy. "Caleb was one of the 10 men that Boaz stopped at the city gate this morning that they might be witnesses of his dealings with Ahira.

"Caleb was curious, of course, as to what the situation was, but when he heard Boaz mention your name, he was really interested. He said that the greed fairly shone on Ahira's face when he heard that Elimelech's land was up for redemption.

"Caleb felt sorry for you and Ruth when Ahira said that he would redeem the land. He said his heart felt like a stone, and that Boaz's face looked absolutely grim.

"But then when Boaz said that Ruth was part of the deal—that whoever bought the land must also be goel for her—then Ahira must have realized that the land would really only be on loan to him, and that in a few years it would be likely to pass on to a son of Ruth.

"Caleb said it was like watching the sun break from behind the clouds to see Boaz's face when Ahira gave his excuses and turned the right of redemption over to Boaz. He said he had never seen a sandal removed and accepted more quickly to seal the matter.

"Then Boaz called on the witnesses and said, 'You are witnesses today that I have bought from the hand of Naomi all that belonged to Elimelech, Mahlon, and Chilion. And I have also acquired Ruth, the Moabitess, the widow of Mahlon, to be my wife in order to carry on the name of the deceased and his inheritance so that the name of Elimelech may not be cut off from his brothers or from his birthplace. You are witnesses today.'

"And all the people around, as well as the 10 called to be witnesses, replied, 'We are witnesses.'

"Then Caleb spoke out in blessing, 'May the Lord make the woman who is coming into your home like Rachel and Leah who built the house of Israel.'

"Someone else said, 'May you achieve wealth in Ephrathah and become famous in Bethlehem.'

"And old Pedahzur said, 'May your house be like the house of Perez whom Tamar bore to Judah, through the children that the Lord will give you by this young woman.'

"Caleb was so excited by it all that he came right home to tell me before going out to the threshing floor." She smiled, remembering his enthusiasm as he had told her the tale.

The women had stopped walking during this recital of the morning's excitement, and Naomi stood transfixed listening. "Oh, Deborah, you make me feel as though I had been there and heard and seen it all. And you were not even there yourself!"

"Ah, but Caleb is not like most men who never remember or tell anything that goes on. He pays attention, and then he tells me all about things. And, of course, what he did not volunteer, I asked, so that I would know just how it was. Are you not glad that I learned the details so that I could pass them on to you?" And she laughed merrily, remembering the inquisition by which she had gained the exact words and actions of each participant in the drama.

Naomi smiled with her. "Yes, indeed, my dear friend. I wish I could have seen it all myself, but with Caleb as a witness and you as a messenger, why should I want for more?"

"I wanted," Deborah continued with sparkling eyes, "to come to your house immediately and give you a report, but Caleb made me see reason. He warned me that I might arrive before Boaz, and how foolish I would appear if Boaz came to tell you the news and found me there ahead of him!"

"I am sure that Caleb is very wise," Naomi agreed with a smile. "Boaz did, indeed, come just before midday. But he certainly did not give us so colorful or detailed an account," she added. "Oh, Deborah, I am so happy for Ruth! Boaz is such a good, kind man, and Ruth will know real security and peace as his wife!" Not even to this dear friend did she tell of her own part and Ruth's in bringing these events to pass. That was a secret belonging to Boaz and Ruth and was theirs to share or not as they chose.

Deborah broke into the small thoughtful lull cheerfully. "And it is no small thing that Boaz is very wealthy. Ruth will never again need to glean in the fields to provide bread for the table."

"No, and I am glad that her life will be easier. But even if he were poor, I would be sure that Boaz was the right one to care for my dear daughter.

"But now," Naomi added, "I must hurry home. The sun is setting, and I have things to do. Thank you for bringing me a full report." Saying their farewells quickly, both women moved off in the direction of their own homes.

Ruth had awakened and was milking the goat when Naomi entered the courtyard. Her eyes were still swollen from sleep, but her face appeared rested.

"Is it well with you, my daughter?" Naomi asked.

"It is well," Ruth replied calmly. "No longer do I feel a need for tears. In fact, in spite of the dusk, my world seems very bright indeed!"

Naomi nodded her understanding. The women prepared their simple meal and ate it with very little attention to the food. Instead, their minds and conversation were full of plans for the future.

"You must have a lovely new robe," Naomi stated decidedly. "When you go to the house of Boaz as his bride, you must look your best. Tomorrow I will go to the house of

Tirzah. She weaves the softest, finest wool in all of Bethlehem. We have enough silver left to buy the material and the wools that I will need to embroider a fine design upon it."

"But, my mother, you must not spend all your silver on a robe for me. And how can you do this embroidery in just one week? I do not need a fancy robe for Boaz. He has accepted me just as I am—a poor gleaner in the fields."

"Yes," Naomi smiled, "he certainly is not taking you for your riches. But you shall have that robe. What need will I have of silver when my daughter is the wife of the wealthy Boaz? And with you here to help with the other work, I will have time to make your robe beautiful."

Then she added, "You are my daughter. Never before have I had the privilege of preparing my daughter for marriage. Please grant me this."

Ruth smiled her understanding and thanks. "Of course, Mother. I will be greatly honored to wear the robe prepared by my mother when I go to the house of my husband, Boaz."

Still planning and chatting, they cleared away the uneaten food and prepared themselves for sleep.

Naomi realized that the following week would be very busy. She had always liked having the days full. She would plan and organize and then, by working together, she was sure that she and Ruth could meet the deadline.

"And now, my God, the Almighty One, I thank You for the events of this blessed day. Thank You for honoring my faith and Ruth's by providing for us so wonderfully. O my Lord, may Your blessing rest upon Boaz and upon Ruth. May You give them children who will bring them honor. May Your holy name also be honored and praised."

17

▼▼▼▼▼▼▼

*T*HE DAYS FLEW BY. Naomi purchased the fabric, white and fine, and immediately began the intricate embroidery that would make it a garment suitable for the bride of a prince. Every spare moment she worked on the robe, occasionally wondering if she had overestimated her ability to work quickly.

While she worked, a steady stream of visitors appeared in the little courtyard. Some were curious to see Ruth, the foreigner who would marry the wealthy and honored Boaz. Others came to rejoice with Naomi. A few came to be unpleasant—to make Naomi understand that she did not deserve this happiness. Naomi quietly agreed with them and added that the Lord was very gracious in blessing His handmaiden.

After the first few callers had come and gone, Naomi realized that she would have to continue to embroider while chatting with the visitors. Otherwise she could never hope to finish the robe in time. And those who came seemed to understand her situation, so the work went on unhindered.

Ruth freed Naomi of much of the routine daily work, efficiently taking over the chores of the house. As she worked, her face was alight with a special glow.

One afternoon, Deborah took her turn among the other visitors. "I just could not stay away," she confessed. "I know that you are busy, but I just had to see you!"

Without giving Naomi a chance to assure her of her welcome, Deborah hurried on, "Everywhere I go I hear of the lovely robe that you are making for Ruth," and she lifted a sleeve to see the beautiful pattern edging it. "It is truly lovely, Naomi, and Ruth will be beautiful wearing it. Of course," she added with a smile directed toward the girl, "she would be beautiful wearing sackcloth, especially in the eyes of Boaz. But this will be much more fitting for the bride of such an honorable man."

Ruth blushed shyly but smiled. Just that morning, she had expressed her concerns to Naomi. She hoped that Boaz would think her beautiful. She could not bear it if he were to be disappointed.

Naomi had reassured her that only a blind man could fail to see her beauty, and that Boaz was certainly not blind. And Boaz had already told her, she reminded the girl, that he considered her to be a very worthy person.

Ruth had replied, "I plan to spend the rest of my life seeing that he is not disillusioned and showing him my gratitude."

Now as Ruth's and Naomi's eyes met, Naomi knew that both were thinking back to that conversation.

One evening, a few days later, Boaz himself arrived in the courtyard. Neither woman was aware of his presence at first, and he studied them a moment before speaking the words of greeting, "Peace be upon you."

Startled, they responded to his greeting with the customary words, "And on you peace."

"It is well," he replied. "And you," he added, "I see that you are very busy. Are you also well?"

"Oh yes, the Lord is blessing each day abundantly."

Conversation was difficult. It was not usual for a woman to entertain a man other than her husband, and the situation was awkward. After a brief interval, Boaz announced his mission.

"Naomi, would you be willing to oversee the wedding feast? Oh, I do not mean the preparation," he added quickly, seeing the sudden dismay on her face. "The servants are handling that well enough. But I have no mother or aunt to watch out for my guests' comfort during the feast. Would you be willing to do that?"

Naomi needed no time to consider her answer. "I am greatly honored, my lord, that you have asked me. It will give me pleasure to do as you ask." And her happy smile showed that her words were spoken in truth.

"Thank you, Naomi. And I also have another request. I would that you reconsider about moving in with us. I would never interfere with your going to the Feast of Tabernacles when the time comes. In fact, perhaps we could all go together. But I fear that you will find it very lonely here by yourself when Ruth is gone."

Naomi felt warmed by his words of concern. It was truly pleasant to have a man to look after her again after these months of being in charge. But she gave him no immediate decision, only promising to consider his words.

Boaz left with the proper farewells, but without ever speaking directly to Ruth. However, that was as it should be. Naomi was glad to observe, though, that his gaze had been often upon the girl and his expression was warm as he watched her.

*　*　*

The great day arrived. At the time of the midday rest, both women were lying on their mats with minds far too busy to allow sleep.

In her mind, Naomi went over the arrangements and activities of the last week. Was everything ready? She had set the last fine stitches in Ruth's delicate wedding garment just before sunset the evening before. Now it lay in regal splendor across the bedding chest.

And Ruth herself lay on her mat, bathed and perfumed with oil, her hair clean and shining. She was ready except for donning the beautiful robe and a final arranging of her hair. How lovely she would look when Boaz came to claim her later this afternoon!

Naomi, too, was bathed and ready to go. Her more sober garments were clean and fresh. She was looking forward eagerly to this wedding feast. Not only would she fill the place of mother of the bride, but also she would fill the place of mother of the groom. Naomi recognized that she was a doer —she would always be happiest if she were busy and needed.

Now Naomi looked around her. Our own house is ready to be left. The jars of grain are tightly covered against mice and insects. The leftover bread has been taken out to the birds. It would be stale when I return at the end of the week—if I do return. It does seem wrong, somehow, to plan to come back to this lonely little house. The only way I can see that it would help anyone would just be the fact of my absence in the house of Boaz. Well, that decision need not be made just now. I will let it rest a few more days.

She pulled her attention back to the checklist in her mind. I must remember to empty the water jar before we leave the house. Everything else—the dried fruit, lentils, and cheese—is safely stored in jars. Yes, inside the house all seems to be ready.

Now, how about outside? A neighbor was glad to have any cucumbers that would be ready during the next week. The lentils and gourds should be all right. And this morning when Zebidah had taken the goat, she had been reminded not to bring it back here, but instead it was to be left with the goats of Caleb for the coming week.

Naomi could think of no task omitted, no item left undone. And while the knowledge gave her joy, she felt a tempering pain at leaving this house. It had seemed such a shabby humble little place when she had first arrived in Bethlehem. But now the walls, the earthen floor, even the hole-filled roof were dear to her.

Again her mind was back on the problem that had been plaguing her. Should I come back alone after the wedding feast? she wondered. Boaz said that she should not.

Deborah had given her another slant on the subject. "The old biddies," she had reported, "are saying that you are going to stay here rather than live with Ruth any longer. They say that you are anxious to be rid of her."

"But, Deborah, you know that it is not true!" Naomi had cried. "How could they say such a thing! I will miss Ruth terribly. I just want to give her a little time alone with her husband before I move in with them."

Ruth had added her own plea one evening before they slept. "My mother, why must you come back here alone? Will you not stay in the house of Boaz with me? You know that I know nothing of managing a large household with many servants. And Boaz has no mother to manage things. You could do that so well."

"Oh, Ruth," Naomi had replied, "that is one reason that I hesitate to live there. I am not the mother of Boaz that I should run his house. I would not take from you the joy of being mistress of your own house. I remember how much I enjoyed being in charge as a bride. I considered it a great challenge to keep the operations of the household running smoothly. Few girls get a chance to be mistress at your age. Usually the husband's mother is in firm control."

"But, Mother, I do not know how to run a house!" Ruth wailed. "I do not think I can do it."

Naomi had smiled at the girl's fears. "But you know how to do all the work of a house. You can see what needs doing. And the servants will love you and be eager to do your bidding. You need not fear, my daughter."

Now as Naomi reflected, she wondered if the girl was right. While I had gloried in managing the servants and keeping my house running efficiently, Naomi remembered, Ruth does not show the same inclinations. She could do it, of course, but would it be a burden to her rather than a privilege? Ruth had always been a willing worker, but never had she assumed leadership. It would be too bad if the first months of marriage were marred for her by unhappiness in the running of the house.

Well, I will see, she thought. I refuse to make the decision today. While I work in the house of Boaz this week during the wedding feast, I will be able to size up the servants and determine whether they would give Ruth trouble.

The afternoon slipped by, and at last Boaz came for his bride. The sight of Boaz in his wedding finery brought a sharp stab of memory to Naomi. Elimelech had been dressed very similarly when he had come to her father's house to claim her as his bride so many years ago.

Naomi smiled warmly at the regal man before her. Boaz's robe, made of a rich blue fabric, was belted with a silken girdle, embroidered with all the lovely colors of the rainbow. His sandals were figured, and the laces, extending up his legs, were carefully and exactly crossed and tied. On his curly dark hair sat a golden crown that proclaimed him an exalted prince, at least for this special day. And all about his person was the fragrance of the frankincense and myrrh with which his garments had been scented.

Boaz returned Naomi's smile a bit sheepishly, and his eyes twinkled. How foolish he feels in that splendid garb! Naomi thought, as she turned back into the house to fetch Ruth.

Within moments Naomi stood in the doorway of the little house, Ruth by her side. The group accompanying Boaz greeted the young Moabitess' appearance with an exuberant cheer. Truly, she was breathtaking. She was dressed in the robe that her mother-in-law had spent so many hours embroidering. She was adorned in jewels and crown, borrowed from Deborah. As she left Naomi's side and stood by her husband-to-be, Naomi caught her breath at the sheer glory of it all. The couple turned and led the rejoicing troop of friends back toward the house of Boaz. There was the music of singing, accompanied by flute and lyre and other instruments of music. Naomi stood a few moments just to savor the joy of this very special day.

With a smile of anticipation, she hurried out of the courtyard and, taking a different route than the bridal procession, almost ran to the house of Boaz. She could still hear the singing and laughter of the procession as she entered the house. Many of the invited guests would join the train as they wound through Bethlehem and would soon arrive, expecting the feasting to begin.

Quickly, Naomi spotted the head servant and reviewed the arrangements. To her relief, everything seemed to be in readiness.

And then the bridal couple was there. Guests were everywhere. The marriage feast was under way.

Through the coming busy days, Naomi was completely in her element. She could remember few weeks that she had enjoyed more. No small part of her joy was the happiness that glowed in the faces of Boaz and Ruth. How she thanked the Lord for the warmth that radiated between them!

But another facet of her pleasure was the thrill of managing a large household in an extremely busy and challenging situation.

All too quickly, the week was over. The guests were gone. The time of decision had arrived. This night Naomi would spend in the house of Boaz. Even now she lay on her pallet, beginning to realize the weariness of her body, but determined to make the decision before she slept.

The house of Boaz is large and luxurious, she reasoned. It would be comfortable to stay here. But would I be expected to sit around, a lady of leisure? That would bring me no pleasure. On the other hand, if I were allowed to take over the management of the house, as I would love to do, would Ruth come to resent my presence eventually?

To go back to my little house would be lonely, but perhaps no more lonely than living among the hustle here and still being alone.

Tonight she felt very lonely, utterly bereft. And it was not just the pain of the spirit; her body also ached to be held by strong arms; her arms longed to hold a husband close. She never had known exactly what led to these attacks of longing. Perhaps tonight it was the consciousness that Ruth lay in the strong, comforting arms of a husband once more. Never again, Naomi acknowledged desolately, will I know that joy. For some moments she lay immersed in her pain.

Then determinedly she sat upright. I will not give in to this loneliness. I have so much—a loving daughter, a wonderfully generous and kind kinsman in Boaz. And they want me. They care about me. And while no one can remedy my deep loneliness, still I need never be all alone.

In my heart I feel that it would be wrong to go back to that lonely little house. The only help I could be to my loved ones there would be simply by my absence. But just this evening Boaz again told me that he wished I would stay on in his house. "I know that Ruth will miss you sorely if you are not here. Not only does she love you as a mother, but also she feels very unsure of handling the servants. Would you not help her and teach her to manage this household?" he had pleaded.

His request had moved her deeply. It is so good to feel needed, Naomi thought joyfully. But aside from all other considerations, Naomi now realized, Boaz is the head of my family line. No longer am I in charge. By becoming goel, Boaz has taken over the duties of leadership for any surviving dependents of his kinsman Elimelech.

At last Naomi realized that only one choice was honorable in her current position. To make any other choice would be another act of rebellion against authority, very like her attitudes in the past.

I will stay, she determined. I will try hard not to intrude into affairs best left to Ruth. And if in time I must sit back and not have an active role in the household, I will concentrate on spinning, weaving, and embroidery. I will not be idle.

At peace with her decision, Naomi turned her thoughts to her God. "O Lord Jehovah, thank You for the redemption that You have provided in the person of Boaz. Thank You for his great tenderness toward Ruth, and for his care for me.

"And now, O Lord, as we enter into our new life here, may we adjust to our new responsibilities. Keep me submissive, Lord, to the one who is now my lord.

"And please, my Father," she added sleepily, "may Ruth be blessed with a fertile womb. May she bear a son to carry on the name of Elimelech and of our son Mahlon."

And at last sleep claimed the weary mind and body of Naomi.

18

⌄⌄⌄⌄⌄⌄⌄⌄⌄

WHEN RUTH LEARNED of Naomi's decision to stay, her joy and relief were so apparent that the older woman felt almost overwhelmed with emotion. How good it is to be loved and needed! But, she vowed silently, I will be very careful not to usurp the position of mistress of the house of Boaz. That is Ruth's position, no matter how willingly she would relinquish the responsibility and honor.

Settling into life in the house of Boaz was more easily accomplished than Naomi had expected. Although Ruth would cheerfully have left all management decisions to her mother-in-law, Naomi insisted that the servants get their orders from the younger woman. Whenever Ruth came to her, uncertain of the best course to be followed, Naomi willingly gave her advice and explained the reasoning behind her suggestions. Thus she was able to be of help while remaining in the background.

The hot days of summer slid by, and the cooler days that warned of the approaching winter took their place. As the month Tishri drew near, Naomi eagerly planned for the trip to Shiloh for the Feast of Tabernacles. At first Boaz and

Ruth had planned to make the trip also, but one day Ruth came to Naomi as she was weaving in the courtyard.

"My mother, I would that you rejoice with me," she opened the conversation. "I am sure that I am with child. The manner of women has not come upon me these two months, and now, also, the smell of food sickens me."

At Ruth's words Naomi's heart leapt like a gazelle. "Oh, my daughter, my heart truly does rejoice with you. May God grant you a son who will bring you great joy. And Boaz— what does he say to this wonderful news?"

"His joy is as great as yours, my mother. And it seems to make no difference to him that this child will carry on the line of Mahlon. He is just bursting with pride.

"But he has decided that I should not go to Shiloh this year. He wants me to guard my health and protect this child. And he says that he will not go to the feast without me. Is there someone else with whom you could travel? We do not want you to miss this trip to Shiloh. I know how much it means to you."

"Oh, my dear Ruth, do not worry about me. I am sure that I can go up with Caleb and Deborah. I will ask them. But I am sorry that you cannot go. I looked forward to your taking part in the celebration and worship there. But, of course, the joy of your news outweighs any sadness that I might feel."

She beamed at the younger woman. "I do not think that the trip would harm you since you are strong and healthy, but I am glad that Boaz treats you with such care. Not all men are so considerate of their wives' comfort and health.

"But, my daughter, now to more immediate matters. Are you able to eat in spite of the sickness?"

"Very little," Ruth admitted reluctantly.

"That is what I thought," Naomi smiled. "I have observed you sitting there, pale and quiet, pretending to eat while the rest of us devour the food. You would do better to stay completely away from the cooking, and also from the meals, and to eat something especially prepared for you. If you would like, I will tell the servants how to prepare some foods that I am sure you will be able to eat. Perhaps an egg cooked gently in water, or a broth of some fowl . . ." And Naomi was on her way, happily planning a meal for the mother-to-be.

So it was that Naomi journeyed to Shiloh in the company of her good friends, Caleb and Deborah. As she had years before, she entered into the spirit of the holiday, enjoying the trip to Shiloh almost as much as the days spent there.

She had brought her remaining silver along, and on the first day that they were at Shiloh, she went to the Tabernacle alone. There she bought a she goat for a sin offering and a young heifer for the peace offering.

First she took the she goat to the priest. As she laid her hands on the goat, in her mind she recounted the sins of weakness and ignorance that she and Elimelech had committed. Then the priest took the animal onto which she had transferred their sins and killed him, catching the blood. After sprinkling the blood upon the horns of the altar, he carefully separated the fat from the meat and entrails of the goat and placed the fat upon the altar. There it burned as a sweet savor to the Lord. The flesh of the goat would be eaten by the priests in the holy place.

Naomi felt a glad release as she watched the fire burn up the fat parts of the animal. The blood of that goat had covered her sins. Now she was truly right with her God.

Then the young heifer was offered for the peace offering. Again Naomi identified the animal with herself by placing her hands on it. After the heifer was killed, its blood, also, was sprinkled upon the altar, and its fat was burned with fire. Then the priest separated the right shoulder and breast. The shoulder was laid aside as the portion for the priest, and the breast was waved before the Lord. The priests would also use the breast as theirs from the Lord. The rest of the meat was given to Naomi. It was hers and must be eaten either today or tomorrow. Any that remained after that time must be burned with fire.

She hurried back to the booth of Caleb and Deborah with the meat. She must prepare it quickly so that it would be ready for the evening meal.

That evening as she ate the meat of the heifer, Naomi's heart was at peace. Truly the Lord was very near to her. He had dealt bountifully with her and she was assured that His bounty would continue as she remained in His "place of blessing." How she rejoiced in the goodness of God!

The days of feasting and rejoicing at Shiloh were full of happiness. Yet, as they started back to Bethlehem, Naomi felt that her heart could rejoice as well anywhere now that she knew this wonderful peace of spirit. Eagerly she walked toward Bethlehem—so much awaited her there.

*　*　*

Back at the house of Boaz everything was focused toward the coming arrival of the baby. Ruth's sprightly step had slowed to the stately tread of a matron. Her body thickened and rounded, and her face wore a glow of contentment.

Boaz fussed over his wife's comfort. Elimelech had been a thoughtful husband, but even he had never shown the concern that Boaz exhibited. Naomi did not understand his worry until one evening he dropped down beside her as she sat in the courtyard.

"Does Ruth seem well to you?" he asked anxiously. "Do you think she is taking proper care? She seems always to be so busy!"

"But, Boaz, she is very well. Just look at her shining eyes! Ruth is a strong, healthy woman and should bear a fine child. I see no need for you to worry." Naomi's voice revealed her puzzlement.

"Perhaps you are right. I pray that you are. It is just that my first wife was delivered of three babies, all before their time. Each died immediately, and each time she was left weaker and more sickly. For many years she was not well, and then just over a year ago she died. When I look at Ruth and realize what might await her, my fears all return." His voice was brusque with the emotion he tried to subdue.

Naomi's heart was moved. No wonder he worried! She tried again to reassure him, and when he left her a little later, she felt that perhaps she had been of some comfort.

Boaz had not told Ruth the reason behind his fears, and Naomi was sure that she should not either. She certainly did not want Ruth to begin to share them.

During the months of waiting, Naomi busily wove soft, fine fabric for the baby. She was glad to have flax to make the linen that would be soft against the tiny baby's skin. Most babies were wrapped in wool, but this child would not have to suffer that.

So the winter months passed while the cold rains kept the women indoors. Even in the large house of Boaz, Naomi felt confined. What would it have been like in the one small room of Cousin Leah's house, especially with the leaking roof?

Then came the spring. The birds appeared and began to build their nests. The men put in busy days in the fields. Since Ruth was heavy with child, Naomi supervised the planting of the garden and then gradually took on more of the work.

At last, one morning a little over a year after their return to Bethlehem, Ruth began her travail. A servant was sent to notify Boaz who was in the fields with his servants. Barley harvest was in full swing, but Boaz had no thought of barley when he received the message. He hurried to his house, only to pace impatiently in the courtyard as the time of travail lengthened. Naomi assured him frequently that all was well, but his fears were not allayed.

Naomi was busily looking after Ruth's comfort. She was delighted to be helping at the birth of this child. She had aided servant women to deliver their babies, but never before had she been the close female relative who oversaw everything and was completely in charge of the event.

The midwife duly appeared and told them all that it would be the final watch of the night or perhaps even the morning before the babe would appear. Ruth groaned at the news, and when Naomi told Boaz the midwife's prediction, she thought that he might faint.

"Do not fear," she reassured him. "This is the way of first babies. Those who open the womb are often very slow at arriving." Then she hurried back to Ruth.

But the midwife was wrong. Just after the sun had set, Ruth gave birth to a son, a perfectly formed child with a lusty cry.

"Oh, my daughter, may God be praised! You have a son!" And after kissing Ruth tenderly, Naomi rushed from the room to tell Boaz.

His relief was so great that once again Naomi feared that he might faint. But he recovered himself and rushed to the door to notify the musicians who waited outside. Immediately the air rang with melody, announcing to all Bethlehem that a son was born in the house of Boaz.

Naomi smiled as she hurried back to mother and babe. If she could shove the midwife aside, she would care for this baby herself.

And indeed, the midwife was still busy with Ruth, so Naomi picked up the unwashed, angrily crying infant. Tenderly she cleansed his body with warm water. Then she rubbed him thoroughly with olive oil and wrapped him securely in the soft linen swaddling clothes that she had woven. When he was securely wrapped, the crying stopped. His little mouth closed, and he slept.

With all the pride of a grandmother, Naomi carried the sleeping infant out for his father's approval. As Boaz looked down at the tiny bundle, tears streamed down his weathered cheeks. His voice was broken as he said, "My son, you will continue the line of my kinsman Elimelech, but you are my son, my dearly beloved son!"

* * *

Eight days later the baby was circumcised. It was a joyous occasion. Friends and relatives gathered to crowd the house of Boaz.

Naomi watched as the proud father displayed his son. After the women had admired the baby, they surrounded Naomi. First one and then another spoke to her in congratulation.

"Blessed is the Lord who has not left you without a redeemer today," said Deborah. "May his name become famous in Israel."

"May he also be to you a restorer of life and a sustainer of your old age," added Mahlah. "For your daughter-in-law, who loves you and is better to you than seven sons, has given birth to him."

Naomi smiled as she replied, "God has truly blessed me. Once again my life is pleasant. The tree has been cast into the waters of Marah, and they are sweet."

She took the sleeping baby from Boaz and held him close in her arms. Her eyes were full of tears of joy. "Oh, my son," she whispered, "what happiness you have brought to me!"

"A son has been born to Naomi," Dinah said reverently. "He should be called Obed."

"Yes, Obed," the other chorused. "Obed, son of Naomi."

* * *

Night had fallen. Naomi lay on her mat, quiet and relaxed. Beside her in his cradle lay little Obed.

Naomi smiled. No longer will my days be empty or filled with weaving. Care of this little one will fill each day to the brim—and the nights, also, often enough, she thought wryly.

And in time he will run and play, and I will be able to guard his steps and keep him from danger. But best of all will be the time when I can teach him the Law of his God. And I will not just teach him the rules and regulations, but the marvelous truth of a God who loves him, a God whom he can trust, no matter what happens or how bad things may look. He will learn to obey the Lord because he loves Him, not just out of fear of punishment. And Boaz will be such a good example of a faithful follower of the true God. And surely this time I will be a true example also.

Ruth and Boaz will probably have other children. And no doubt, I will, also, share in their care. The house will ring with happy voices and laughter of children, but this child will always be special. Only he will carry on the line of Elimelech.

As Naomi looked into the now bright future, her thoughts turned to the One who had made all this possible. Oh, how good the Lord has been. It is as if all the events, all the sorrows of my life have led to just this moment.

"O my God, how can I thank You for this wonderful gift—this sign of Your love and forgiveness! O my Father, while I will always miss my husband Elimelech, no longer am I alone. I have this child. As with Job, you have brought me through the trials and have now blessed me abundantly!

"May I be faithful in teaching Obed Your Word. May I show him by my life the true meaning of obedience to Your Law.

"O Lord God of Israel, protect this child Obed. May he always serve the God of his father Elimelech. May he trust You and know Your blessing.

"My Lord, I thank You . . ."

And Naomi slept with her hand on the cradle of little Obed.

Glossary

Azaz—Hebrew word meaning "strong"

Bethlehem—the word literally means "house of bread," more loosely interpreted as "place of blessing"

Ephah—about four-fifths of a bushel

Feast of Tabarnacles—an annual seven-day celebration observed in the autumn, during which the Israelites were to live in booths made of branches, remembering the Lord's care for them during their 40 years of wandering in the wilderness; many special offerings were also included in the festivities.

Goel—the Hebrew word for kinsman-redeemer

Homer—10 ephahs or about 8 bushels

Kinsman-redeemer—a brother or near relative of a deceased man who was obligated by the law to marry the deceased's widow. The first child of this union would inherit the deceased's property.

Mara (Marah)—a Hebrew word meaning "bitter" (Exod. 15:23-25)

Mattock—a tool for loosening earth, shaped much like a pickax, but having one side blunt rather than pointed

Naomi—Hebrew word meaning "pleasant"

Tishri—the seventh month of the Hebrew calendar, corresponding to the period from mid-September to mid-October on our modern calendar

Scripture Quotations

Bibliography

Buksbazen, Victor. *The Gospel in the Feasts of Israel.* W. Collingswood, N.J.: The Spearhead Press, 1954.

Eerdmans' Family Encyclopedia of the Bible. Grand Rapids: Wm. B. Eerdmans Publishing Co., 1978.

Everyday Life in Bible Times. Washington, D.C.: National Geographic Society, 1967.

Great People of the Bible and How They Lived. Pleasantville, N.Y.: The Reader's Digest Association, Inc., 1974.

Hession, Roy. *Our Nearest Kinsman.* Fort Washington, Pa.: Christian Literature Crusade, 1976.

Klinck, Arthur W. *Home Life in Bible Times.* St. Louis: Concordia Publishing House, 1969.

LaSor, William Sanford. *Daily Life in Bible Times.* Cincinnati: Standard Publishing, 1966.

Mackie, George M. *Bible Manners and Customs.* Old Tappan, N.J.: Fleming H. Revell Co., 1898.

The Sacred Land. Philadelphia: A. J. Holman Co., 1966.

Unger, Merrill F. *Unger's Bible Dictionary.* Chicago: Moody Press, 1962.

Wight, Fred H. *Manners and Customs of Bible Lands.* Chicago: Moody Press, 1974.